MW01520230

Definitely You

WILLOWBROOK LAKE

BOOK TWO

ASHLEY ERIN

Definitely You

Copyright © 2024 by Ashley Erin

Cover Design by Designs by Dana

Image from Deposit Photos

Developmental Editing: M.E. Carter

Editing: Missy Borucki

Proofreading: Virginia Tesi Carey

Sensitivity Reading: T.C.

Interior Design: Ashley Erin

All rights reserved. No part of this book may be reproduced or transmitted in any form or by any means, electronic or mechanical, including photocopying, recording, or by any information storage and retrieval system, without permission in writing.

No part of this work was generated or aided with the use of AI.

This is a work of fiction. Names, characters, places and incidents are the product of the author's imagination or are used fictitiously, and any resemblance to any actual persons, living or dead, events, or locales is entirely coincidental. The author acknowledges the trademarked status and trademark owners of various products referenced in this work of fiction, which have been used without permission. The publication/use of these trademarks is not authorized, associated with, or sponsored by the trademark owner. All rights reserved.

❀ Created with Vellum

Dedicated to Katrina.
Thank you for encouraging me.
Cheering me on.
And believing in me.

Prologue

RAELYNN
Five Years Ago

My throat is tight as I toss the test into the trash. Negative. Again.

We've been trying for eighteen months to conceive, and once again, we've failed. The hole in my heart is aching as I brush the tears away and touch up my makeup.

The last time I broke down in front of Cam trying to explain my grief, I could see how much it hurt him, and he shut down for days after. Some new game taking his full attention. I can't go through that again, have him pull away. It hurts more than all the negative tests combined.

When there's no trace of the anguish on my face, I rejoin him in the living room. He looks up at me, his face shifting into one of hope when he sees my face clear of the emotions boiling inside me. Sitting next to him, I shake my head. "It was negative."

He sighs, the hope falling and his hazel eyes dim. "That sucks, but we can keep trying if you want."

My heart sits heavy in my chest. He doesn't understand the anguish. Every month, my hope builds that maybe it's this month. Maybe we can finally celebrate together, the frayed edges of our relationship mended. I figured kids would come someday, and I know Cam has always wanted to be a dad. I've had this idea in my head of the family we would create together. We've dreamed of it and talked about it for almost as long as we've been together. He continues to play his game, and almost through a fog, I hear him ask what we should have for dinner.

My throat constricts and it feels like I'm suffocating. This endless loop of hope and disappointment. The whittling away at our relationship. I look over at Cam and at this moment, he's not the man I love. The man with whom I have built a vision of a future. He's a man who is a walking reminder of what I can't and will never have. The person I have continuously failed for a year and a half.

I can't do it.

This endless disappointment, feeling like I can't share with him how I'm feeling about it without hurting him, it's too much. Somewhere in this journey to build a family, we lost *us*.

"Cam, I can't. I can't do this anymore. Trying to get pregnant. Us. It's not working, any of it." My words come out emotionless, everything locked up tight. My mind is a black pit of despair, and sitting with him only drags me down deeper. At least this way he can get out.

I stand up before he can say anything and walk out the door of our apartment without looking back. I know he will try to stop me, to say it's okay, but it's not. I can't keep shielding him from this hurt because it's broken me, us.

CHAPTER
One

RAELYNN

My phone dings, and an alert pops up, letting me know I have a match on the newest dating app I'm trying. Adeline and Elise convinced me it was a good idea, but until today I haven't bothered to do anything with it.

The client I'm showing hems and haws as he pulls out his measuring tape for the fifth time since we got to the house an hour ago.

This is the only reason the app was opened today. It's been like this at nearly every house, and whenever I try to talk to him about the features of the home, he ignores me.

Checking the alert, I see Caleb has already sent me a message.

Glancing over at where Bill jots a note on his legal pad, I open the message.

> Hey! I'm glad we matched! I'm new in town and was excited to see someone as witty and beautiful as you appear on my feed. You said you're a Realtor. I always thought that would be an interesting job.

Pulling up his profile, I'm drawn in by his friendly smile, dark skin, and the fade he's rocking is sexy as fuck. Willowbrook Lake is fairly diverse for a small town, but I'm one of only a handful of Black women in town. My dad has lived here his entire life and my Momma moved here from Jamaica when they met on vacation and fell in love. This town accepted them back when biracial couples were still uncommon, but it's nice to see that we're attracting more people of color. I know it's a passion of my mother's. She works hard to ensure Willowbrook Lake is inclusive, and she does a damn good job of it. The mayor even formed a committee that she heads. Every so often, I participate in the things she plans, but it's her baby and I only help when asked.

His bio describes him as hard working, up for adventure, and looking to meet like-minded people. It doesn't give a lot, but his smile definitely grabs my attention. As much as I dread the idea of dating, I long for the kind of love I've only known once. Maybe it's time, time to finally move on.

> Right now, I'm with a client measuring each room several times in the past hour, so it's thrilling. What do you do?

The little bubbles pop up right away.

I'm a firefighter. I typically work with the wildfire team, but recently took a position here in town. Why don't we meet for drinks later? I would love to chat in person, I'm not really fond of small chat over text.

"I think I'm done here." My client stands, finally addressing me. "I'm just not sure. Can we go see that first place again later this week?"

Sliding my phone in my purse, I pull up the calendar on my work phone. This will be the third time he's seen the first place.

"Let me confirm with the selling Realtor and I will book a time." Shooting off a message, I follow him out and lock up.

He gets in his car with a wave. Sighing as he drives away, I turn off my work phone and stretch. It's been a crazy Monday and after all the fires I had to put out between showings, I deserve a coffee and treat from Perk Up. It's already way past dinnertime and I haven't eaten since breakfast.

Things I used to love about my day no longer hold the same appeal they once did. If I'm being honest with myself, my passion for real estate has been waning for a couple years. I long for more stable hours and income. I do well, but I work damn hard for it at the sacrifice of my personal life. Especially in a town as small as Willowbrook Lake. I've been trying to balance my life more and have definitely felt it financially. The idea of starting a new career in my thirties is terrifying, which is the only reason I haven't taken the plunge.

Breathing in deeply, I recite the positives of my job. Flexible hours, the ability to earn large chunks of money all at once, and the creative side of staging homes. I've been repeating these more frequently recently, and they are not as effective as they once were.

It starts to snow as I drive along Main Street. Big huge flakes. I love each season in my little town, but there's something so magical about winter. The town gets quieter, the tourist season is over, and everything slows down.

Parking, I hop out of my car. There's a freshness in the air that only comes with snow. Closing my eyes, I tilt my head back, the slight breeze biting at my cheeks. All the tension from the day fades. Letting my breath out, I watch as the cloud of air dissipates before making my way into Perk Up.

Elise looks up from the counter when the bell rings, announcing my entrance, and smiles. Grinning in return, I glance around the packed shop, my smile growing when I see Adeline and Owen sitting at a small table, leaning into each other. Adeline looks a little flustered while Owen watches her intently. That man is falling hard for her. I hope it goes somewhere. Adeline glances my way, flushing even more when I wink at her before making the short distance to the counter.

"You look like you could use a cup of coffee." Elise starts on my regular flat white. "Rough day?"

Nodding, I sigh. My day hit the ground running with a sale falling through because the sellers weren't willing to meet my clients halfway on the purchase contract. All my clients wanted was for them to make a significant repair found during the inspection or drop the price to cover it.

So, we have to start from scratch, and they can only meet in the evenings or on Saturdays.

"Yeah, started rough with a sale falling through. And this one client finds something wrong with every single house. Like the one house we looked at, he didn't like that the trim on the main floor doesn't match the trim on the second floor."

She tsks empathetically as she hands me my coffee. "That sucks, I'm sorry. You haven't been loving work lately and I hate to see it. Have you thought more about transitioning to something new? You used to love graphic design. Or what about that coaching opportunity?"

"I have been thinking about the real estate coaching, but it doesn't really get me fired up. I love graphic design, but I would be starting from scratch and I just don't know if I'm ready to take the leap." She's not wrong; both of those are things I've been thinking about exploring, but I just haven't been able to make myself seriously contemplate it, and the fear of the unknown is stopping me.

She hands me my coffee. "It's never too late to find your passion."

"Thank you." Taking the coffee, I sip and relax even more. "Can I also get a cream-cheese filled blueberry muffin, please? And you're right, it's never too late. It doesn't mean it's not scary."

As she turns to get the muffin, the bell rings.

Elise hands it over. "No charge today."

Glaring, I shake my head. "If you think I'm leaving without paying, you have another think coming. Ring me up now."

She scowls in return but knows better than to argue

with me. Bending my head, I select a generous tip and tap my card to pay.

Looking up, my "thank you" falters when I see Elise's worried expression as she looks at me and then back at the door.

Turning, my entire world freezes when I see who's at the door.

Cameron.

His brown hair is buzzed close to his head, vastly different than the last time I saw him. He used to keep it on the longer side, with waves curling around his ears. Closing my eyes for a moment, I let myself remember the feeling of his soft hair running through my fingers. They twitch at the memory before balling into fists, my nails biting into the skin of my palms.

The threat of tears stings my eyes, so I press my nails harder into my skin and force a smile. It's been five years, but the hurt and the pain still feel as fresh as the day I ended our relationship. His expression is fierce, an intensity I don't remember ever crossing his face except for the day I called it quits.

My stomach sinks, and I glance behind him, dreading meeting his wife under these circumstances, but there's no one there.

Every pair of eyes in the room is on me and you could hear a pin drop. I feel their gazes pressing down on me almost as much as Cam's. Everything around the room blurs as I struggle to stand tall.

Sipping my coffee, I adjust my purse as I attempt to make my face neutral. I knew this day might come, but after five years, I thought I was in the clear. The man that I tossed aside is burning holes into the top of my head as I stall.

With a deep breath I meet his gaze and move forward. My feet feel heavy, but I push on until I'm stopped in front of where he blocks the door, not moving to let me pass. "Hi, Cameron." My voice sounds weak to my ears. "It's been a long time."

"It has, Rae." His deep voice is quiet, soft. But I feel its weight in my chest. The urge to throw myself in his arms is strong. No other arms have felt as good as his. His hugs were always able to put me back together and part of me wishes this situation was no different.

Breathing in, I freeze. That was a mistake as his familiar scent takes over my senses. My heart feels the pull it always has in his presence. I'm frozen, words abandoning me as I soak in his presence wanting to stay in this moment while also wishing I could be anywhere else.

His eyes flick between mine, searching. The tension builds in the silence as everyone in the room stares. Somewhere in the pounding of my heart in my ears, I hear a few people tapping on their phones. That sound helps ground me enough to know that soon the entire town will know he's here.

Before we can say anything else, my phone rings. Relief eases the pressure on my chest. "Excuse me, I have to take this."

Skirting around him, I rush out the door and run to my truck. The phone cuts out as Elise hangs up, her special ringtone fading.

My phone beeps as a barrage of messages come in. I know it's Elise and Adeline, but I throw everything into my car, somehow managing to hold onto my coffee and get in. Blindly, I buckle up and make my way home.

Why is he here?

Oh god, please tell me his wife isn't here too and was just at the inn or something. I couldn't handle seeing them together, living the life I imagined I would share with him. I've seen photos of her. And him. Looking happy and in love. I don't need to see it in real life.

Before I can process the drive, I'm parked in my driveway. Head spinning, I gather everything and head into the house.

My entire body feels weighted, emotions flooding through me as I toss my things onto the table, only thinking to grab my phone when it beeps again. Mocha watches me instead of greeting me like usual until I collapse on the couch.

Everything I have tried to overcome in the past five years comes crashing down. Not that I've made huge strides, I definitely regress with every failed attempt at meeting someone new, but seeing him in person was potent.

The smell of his cologne, that same soft panty-melting scent he wore when we were together, lingers like he's still in the room. Memories of our life together are sweet torture as I gather Mocha into my arms and cry into her fur.

All the regret that's sat heavy in my mind over the past years spills out. "What did I do? Why does it still have to hurt so damn much?" Sobbing into her fur, I soak in her comfort as she meows in response.

We had the perfect love, high school sweethearts that fit

together like puzzle pieces. Everything was perfect until the toll of trying to conceive broke me down into a shell of the person I used to be. And I could see the pain it caused Cameron to see me struggling. It was too much for us.

There's a knock on my door before the keypad beeps and the front door opens.

James sits next to me, gathering me into his arms before I've even processed who it is.

"Rae Rae." His voice is soothing.

He sits with me, letting me cry out all the reawakened emotions until I have nothing left.

Leaning back, I gaze at my brother through puffy eyes. His dark eyes are worried, the shoulders of his uniform darkened by my tears.

We've always been close, but the past several years have brought us even closer. He knows everything about everything, right down to the way my relationship with Cameron haunts me.

"It's okay." I straighten my shoulders. "This is his hometown. He has every right to be here. My inability to live with the decision I made is my problem. It just reminds me how much work I have to do to let go. I was just surprised to see him."

His expression is somber as he watches me blow my nose. Skepticism colors his voice as he stands. "If you say so. I'm going to make you something to eat."

Wiping my eyes, I ground myself before joining him in the kitchen. I'm strong. I can handle this.

"No, it's okay. I have a date. I just need to make myself presentable—and confirm." Giving a dry chuckle, I ignore the raised brows.

Seeing Cam in the flesh and knowing he's moved on just fuels my need to be okay. Opening the app, I type a quick message to Caleb confirming and sending a time to meet.

James hands me a glass of water as I put my phone away. "Are you sure you're in the headspace to meet someone?"

"Now is as good a time as any." My voice is surprisingly strong as the reality of what I've done sinks in.

Holy shit, I'm going on a date.

CHAPTER
Two

CAMERON

The sign for Willowbrook Lake makes reality set in. I haven't returned to the town I grew up in since Raelynn ended our thirteen-year-long relationship, crushing my heart in the process. It was too painful to come back. Whenever I contemplated the idea, I would imagine running into Rae and it was too much.

Yet here I am, five years later. Returning home to the place I both love and loathe. The home that holds my happiest memories and my worst.

The bright November sun shines in, making the gold band on my left hand glint. Slowing to a stop as a horse and rider cross the road, I slide the band off and toss it into the center console. It's been on there for months, and I never got used to it. Sarah and I knew early in our marriage that we made a mistake. It took one conversation about our future to decide our fate.

Parking outside Perk Up, I brace myself for the small town chatter before getting out of my vehicle. I head inside, the sight of Raelynn at the counter halting me in my tracks. Her hair is curly and natural, the way I always loved it.

After a moment, she turns, seeing me and I can't tear my eyes away from her as she makes her way over. Those beautiful brown eyes have the same hold on me they always did. It doesn't matter that I haven't seen her in five years. My body still remembers. Our interaction is a blip, the sear on my heart stings as the door shuts loudly behind Raelynn. The café is silent, with all eyes on me. Meeting Owen's gaze, I nod without smiling. He's looking at me with sympathy, but he's sitting with a pretty woman, and I don't feel like exchanging pleasantries with someone I don't know. Not after that.

With a sigh, I head to the counter. "Hey, Elise."

Her smile is genuine, but I see the worry in her eyes. I haven't spoken to Rae since we broke up. If I'm being honest, I distanced myself from most of our friends, which was hard. I didn't want the temptation to ask about Rae, especially once I was dating Sarah. The exceptions were Owen and Young Jae. Even after all the years apart, we managed to stay close.

It was hard though. Rae unfriended me on all social media platforms when I met Sarah, although I can't blame her for that. If our roles were reversed, I would've done the same.

"Hi, Cameron. How are you?"

Returning Elise's smile, I shrug. "I've been better, but it'll work itself out."

Ordering, I drop a twenty on the counter. I can feel all the eyes in the room burning into me, the space eerily silent as Elise makes my coffee. I knew this was coming, but I feel like a caged animal. Living in a big city these past five years made me take anonymity for granted. Elise passes me my coffee, a bit of the worry leaving her gaze when she sees me shifting in place.

"Thank you." I nod, turning and escaping with a quick goodbye. A mere five or six minutes have passed since I walked in the door, but it feels like an eternity.

As resentful as I am that Raelynn gave up on us without even giving me a reason, seeing her up close again reminds me why I came back. I either need closure once and for all, or these feelings aren't meant to go away and I need to show her we can work through everything from the past five plus years.

Not wanting to head home, I walk along Main Street. A few people greet me as I walk, but there are some unfamiliar faces too. The town has definitely grown, but its core has not changed at all.

Finishing my coffee, I toss the cup into a bin and head to the market. Might as well grab some groceries while I try to process seeing Rae again.

Her familiarity hasn't faded even after all this time. Her dark hair falling in those beautiful curls around her face a little longer than the last time I saw her, but otherwise she looks almost the exact same. The warmth of her brown skin was complemented by the pink coat she was wearing. I remember how soft her skin always was. Her glistening eyes and emotion-filled voice were a gut punch. I never expected such an expression of hurt to be directed at me. Wasn't she the one who called it quits? I never wanted to be with anyone but her. She made that choice.

My chest tightens as anger and sadness fight each other. That expression made me want to pull her into my arms, but I also wanted to ask how she dared to look at me like I was the one who tore us apart when she did that with her own words.

They still cut like a knife.

Cam, I can't. I can't do this anymore. Trying to get pregnant. Us. It's not working, any of it.

Throwing things into my basket, I don't really pay attention to what I'm buying as a clerk I don't recognize, scans everything and I pay.

Leaving the market, I shake my head. I need answers.

"Cameron?"

Turning, I see Young Jae holding a bag from Hank's Hardware. Chuckling, I mutter, "I forgot how small this town is. How are you?"

"Good. Man, it's great to see you." He walks over and gives me a hug. "How long are you here for? We need to catch up."

Gesturing to one of the benches that lines the street, we brush the snow off and sit. "I just bought the clinic from Suzanne. I'm here to stay."

His eyes widen. "That's great!" He glances at my bare hand but doesn't say anything. "Where's Sarah?"

"Sarah is at her house. We finalized our divorce this month." He's the first person I've told, outside my family, but it's going to come out eventually.

He claps his hand on my shoulder. "I'm sorry."

I lean back and sigh. "Honestly, it's for the best. It didn't take long after the wedding to realize we got married for the wrong reasons. I started the process of buying the clinic and finalized the deal the day after the divorce was done. There's more for me here and I needed to come home. It was time."

He stares at me, his intensity heavy as he reads between the lines. "I see." He glances at his watch. "I'm sorry. I told my parents I would be back by now to help them with a repair. You should come to my annual winter cabin getaway. The entire crew is coming, but there's more than enough room for you too."

"I don't know. Do you need an answer now? Or can I think about it and get back to you." I want to go, being in close quarters with Rae is tempting, but I don't know if the timing is right.

He nods. "Of course. Let me know."

We say our goodbyes before standing and going our separate ways. A couple weeks away with Raelynn right there would be interesting, but I'm not letting her get away without an explanation again and I don't want to make things uncomfortable for our friends.

Glancing at the stores as I pass, I pause at the bank. A flier for the Willowbrook Lake Masquerade Ball fills part of the window, boasting that it's going to be bigger and better than ever. The charity this year is the animal shelter, a great cause. The annual event is one Rae and I used to love. It might be worth going and reconnecting with my town roots.

———

Heading back to my car, I make the rest of the way to the vet clinic I just purchased. Suzanne, the previous owner, reached out to me personally when she decided to sell. She was the one who gave me my start in the field, hiring a gangly teenage boy to help around the place and teaching me in the process. I couldn't say no. Not that I wanted to.

Pulling into the empty parking lot, I'm glad I decided to wait until the purchase was finalized to arrive. It will help keep me busy as I adjust to being back.

I eye the attached house, which is also now mine. It's small, but more than enough for me until I find a more permanent spot. I know exactly the house I want; I just need to find out if the owners will sell it.

Suzanne comes out, her warm smile a balm to the rawness still stinging from seeing Raelynn. The wild waves surrounding Suzanne's face are a bit grayer than they used to be. There are smile lines around her brown eyes, but aside from that, she looks almost the same as she did the day I let her know I was leaving.

Hopping out of my car, I shut the door and stride into her waiting arms. "Suzanne! It's wonderful to see you."

Her embrace feels like coming home as much as seeing the town sign and driving down Main Street did.

"Cameron, my boy. It's been far too long." Her voice carries a small note of admonition, but mostly I hear the barely contained tears. "Welcome home."

Squeezing her tightly, I inhale the scent of her floral perfume mixed with the chemicals she cleans the clinic with. "I know. But I'm here to stay."

Suzanne releases me, holding me at arm's length to do her assessment. "Looks like you've been taking care of yourself." Her eyes narrow as she scans my face, admonishing, "Except you're not sleeping."

"It's been a hard couple weeks wrapping up the divorce and getting all that settled. Then dealing with the purchase of the clinic. I wanted to get here to handle it all in person, but packing up a house and separating things took longer than I anticipated." Shrugging, I wrap my arm around her waist and we walk into the clinic together.

It looks exactly the same as I remember. A small waiting room with two armchairs and a loveseat. The nook designated for dog and cat food, over-the-counter medications, and other supplies off to the side of the reception desk.

The four exam rooms line the hallway to the back, where the operating room, grooming center, bathroom, and office are all housed.

"It feels like I haven't been gone a day. This place hasn't changed at all!" Admiration colors my voice. Incredibly, Suzanne has run this clinic for close to twenty-five years and it's still in immaculate condition. A huge testament to the love and pride she has put into it.

We go over the transition plan. Suzanne will stay on for six months before retiring, but she's already notified the clients of the clinic that she has sold it to me and will be transitioning slowly by reducing her hours and moving into a more supportive role. Since I left, she's hired three staff; a vet tech, an administrative assistant, and a groomer. I will meet them tomorrow.

"Are you sure you don't want to take some time to

settle in before getting to work?" Suzanne's brows knit in worry as she unlocks a door at the very rear of the clinic and leads me into the adjoining house.

"I'm sure. The moving van with most of my things won't be here until Friday, so I don't have much to do anyway." Kicking off my shoes, I take in the laundry room. It's a good size and I like that it's right off the clinic. It will be nice not to walk through the house in dirty scrubs at the end of a hard day.

Attached to the laundry room is the living room. It's small but more than enough for my small sectional and TV. I didn't hang onto much after everything was settled, less to move and easier to start fresh.

The main floor is open concept, with the kitchen to the front of the house. It has a ton of cabinets and a massive island to prep. A small but functional pantry and a half bath are off to the side.

Upstairs has a massive primary bedroom with a stunning en suite and a smaller bedroom with an attached bath as well.

"I was renting it to my old vet tech before she returned to school. She left behind her bedroom furniture because she was moving into a furnished suite. I believe the mattress is fairly new."

"It's perfect." I'm glad for the apartment, it's tough to find vacant ones in Willowbrook Lake since the town is so small.

We head back down the stairs and into the clinic.

"Why don't you come for dinner tonight? I know Hank would be glad to see you." Suzanne grabs her things from the office that now belongs to me.

I wrap an arm around her and walk her out. "That sounds great."

After she drives away, I look around the empty parking lot before really taking in the clinic. It was always my dream to take it over from Suzanne. I never thought I would be here after the past five years, but this clinic, like Willowbrook Lake, is where I'm supposed to be.

CHAPTER
Three

RAELYNN

Caleb opens the door to the restaurant, holding it open for me and the couple behind us. He suggested going to a restaurant in the town over, something I jumped on. Despite the headspace I was in making this date, Caleb instantly puts me at ease as he sits across from me.

"I saw one of the houses you have listed for sale. They really did an impeccable job decorating the outside of the home. It makes me want to see the inside." His gaze is warm as he leans back in the booth.

Grinning, I sit up a little straighter. "That was me. Since they were selling, they didn't want to put in the effort, but I convinced them to let me. The outside of the home is fairly cookie-cutter, but the inside is immaculate. I wanted the outside to reflect how beautiful the inside is."

Our server comes before he can respond, and I admire

how polite and respectful he is. She's clearly new and nervous, but he doesn't get impatient with her. She takes our drink orders and leaves.

"You have a great eye for design." He continues the conversation seamlessly.

"Thank you."

Our drinks are served and things continue to flow easily between us, but there's no spark. I like talking to him and enjoy his company, but the vibes I'm getting aren't romantic.

"I know you mentioned getting a position here, but was there something more that led to the decision to move to our small town? Don't get me wrong, it's great; it's just a quiet scene compared to what it sounds like you're used to." Switching the attention from myself, I sip my iced tea, pausing as his eyes shutter.

His smile falls. "It was just time for a fresh start."

Awkward silence falls between us for the first time, and the server comes up to take our order as I shift. Despite the change in his mood, Caleb continues to act in a way that I admire, he gestures to me to order first and compliments our server on how well she remembers the specials.

"I tried serving at a restaurant for about a week. I told a table we had something on special that wasn't even on the menu," he quips.

She laughs, jotting down his order.

He leans toward me, his expression contrite. "I'm sorry I was a bit short. Things with my ex didn't end well, and I don't really like thinking about the last six months before I moved."

"I get it. Breakups suck."

We move past the awkwardness, enjoying the rest of our dinner.

As we finish dessert, Caleb smiles at me. "I enjoyed myself. Would you like to do it again?"

Taking a deep breath, I give him a small smile. "I would—as friends."

Caleb returns my smile, his demeanor staying the same. "Sounds great. I can always use a friend."

———

For the next two weeks the entire town is talking about Cam and the fact he's here to stay. No one knows much, and anyone who has information on why he's here and why his wife hasn't joined him yet has been tight-lipped.

Entering the beauty salon, I greet Tamarya with a fond hug. She opened the salon about seven years ago and has been incredible in ordering products meant for my hair.

"Hey, love. The curl cream you like just arrived and I made sure to order in more shampoo and conditioner." She gestures to the section of products meant specifically for curly hair. Seeing the stocked shelves, I do a little shimmy.

"That's amazing! Thank you!" The first time I came in, she didn't have any products that worked well for my hair, something she not only immediately recognized, but also corrected right away. Not only that, she began taking classes on the proper ways to cut and treat my hair so I didn't have to travel two hours away to get it done. It's one of the things I truly appreciate about her. She has gone above and beyond to ensure her collection is inclusive.

I browse, picking up some of my usual before stopping

at a new line of makeup. "The shade range in these foundations is incredible!"

Snapping a photo, I send it to my mom. She's always struggling to find a foundation dark enough. James took after our mom more than our dad, the tone of his skin much deeper than mine.

"I hear you went out with the new firefighter?" Tamarya comes over, leaning against the wall as I browse.

Scoffing, I glance at her. "Somehow you heard about that even though we met outside of town, but I still don't know why Sarah hasn't joined Cam here yet. If people are going to gossip, it would be nice if they could be more informative."

She gasps. "Oh my, you didn't hear. They're not together anymore. Cam's divorced."

I almost drop the bottle I'm holding, my heart kicking into high gear. "What?"

Tamarya starts to tell me what she's learned, but I have a hard time focusing. My ears are ringing and there's a cacophony of emotions flooding through me. So many I can't even begin to process any except the feeling of relief.

CHAPTER
Four

RAELYNN

Adding one final swipe of mascara, I head into my bedroom to put on my gown. The town's annual masquerade ball is tonight and I look forward to this event every year. The only one I missed was the one right after Cameron and I ended our relationship.

The material of the floor-length gown slides over my skin, the satiny fabric has a soft shimmer to it that will almost glow under the lighting at the hall. The skirt is deep green with a sheer black overlay that has little diamond beads sewn throughout layered on top. It flows out from my hips to drape flawlessly to the floor around my feet, swishing when I walk. The bodice has the same layered look but fitted tightly to my body. The V-neckline amplifying my pushed-up cleavage. The straps are green vines with beading that drape over my shoulders to twist together down my spine where the skirt rests on my lower back.

Sliding into my shoes, a simple black stiletto, I grab my clutch and mask and head out after a quick goodbye to Mocha.

Considering the small size of Willowbrook Lake, the town hall is huge, but it needs to be because when events like this happen, everyone shows up. The rustic building is covered in fairy lights and dense greenery. It's fitting since the theme this year is Fae Royalty.

People stream inside, gowns, suits, and everything in between create a stunning sight of creativity and elegance.

Somehow I manage to find a parking space fairly close to the entrance. I do a quick makeup check before grabbing my mask. Positioning it just right, I weave it through my curls before clipping it in place to make a pretty updo. The mask is intricate, a spirally base in black underneath a detailed design of green, crystally vines that twist away from the mask into pretty purple flowers.

Checking my phone, I smile when I see a message from Elise letting me know that she's inside and secured our group a table. My heart flutters as I join the crowd of people entering the building.

The inside of town hall looks even more magical than the outside. Somehow the committee created a fairy forest that feels incredibly real. Trees, toadstools, birds, butterflies, and flowers of all sizes and colors decorate the room. The lighting is more twinkling fairy lights hanging in strands from the vaulting ceiling.

The tables line the exterior walls on the outside of the forest with little gaps to provide a view of the dance floor centered in the middle. The décor around the tables is simpler, but just as magical. Sheer green drapes hang above them and down the walls, lights shining through them.

The food is set up in one of the smaller halls to the side, with people already in and out with plates of delicious goodies catered by Willow's Catering.

Music fills the dimly lit space, drowning out the sound of voices as the DJ plays some dance remix. Looking around, I spot the DJ on one of the mezzanine levels, out of sight so not to distract from the magic of the room.

Weaving through the crowd of people, smiling and saying hi as I go, I find the table Elise snagged for us. Every year, we try to see how long it takes for people to recognize each other. The only exception to that rule is the women in our group always shop together. This year we got to introduce Adeline to the mix, and it's been so wonderful.

Elise sees me first, her squeal of delight drowning out even the music. She looks stunning in a beautiful blue and gold dress. The skirt flows around her legs in swaths of fabric that look almost like feathers. The bodice of her dress a deep plunging halter style. I don't know how she's supporting herself, but everything stays put as she rushes toward me.

"Oh. My. God! You look amazing!" She hugs me, holding me close when I try to pull away. Her voice is low, concerned. "Cameron is here and grabbing food. Are you going to be okay?"

Licking my lips, I nod. That fluttering in my heart returning. Ever since seeing him at Perk Up we haven't run into each other. But I've heard all the buzz. He bought the vet office and moved back home without Sarah.

He's divorced.

Tamarya told me the news days ago and I'm still riding through the emotions. The masochistic side of me that's held on to hope we would get another chance is elated. The more realistic side of me has been rationally convincing myself we can move past our history and be friends.

"Yeah, he's here to stay. We will figure it out. It's been five years. I was just shocked when I saw him." Smiling, I can feel the strain in my jaw, but I know it will get easier the more I'm exposed to him.

Her gaze is concerned, but she nods before her eyes brighten again when she looks over my shoulder.

Turning, I see Young Jae approaching us looking devastatingly handsome in all black. His suit is pristine and fitted perfectly to his body. His black and gold mask is molded into the shape of a crown. It's masculine and sexy.

Turning back to her, I glance around us and notice someone missing. "Where's Jake?"

Her elated expression falls for a moment. Sighing, she says, "He isn't feeling well and decided to stay home. I hate to say it, but I think feeling sick was just an excuse not to come."

I give her a side hug and turn to watch Young Jae as he stops to talk to someone. Elise hasn't said anything since she talked to me and Adeline at the lake, but I can sense that things with Jake are still strained. She works hard not to vent her frustrations, but whenever I go to their place, I've seen little signs that not all is well in her world.

"His loss," I murmur. Biting back my grin, I watch Young Jae finish his conversation and beeline it straight to Elise. His feelings for her are obvious to everyone but the two of them. And as Elise's face lights up once again, I don't think it's one-sided. Sighing, I turn and grin when I see Adeline and Owen. They look amazing, their outfits complementing each other.

Adeline gives a wave before she notices Elise and Young Jae, the same knowing look I'm sure I just had flashes as she grins. Smiling, I weave around the table, hugging her, I take the seat next to where she's standing, pulling out the one next to me. She sits down with a grateful look. Owen wanders off to greet someone. Adeline angles her chin back to the oblivious duo.

"History there?" She gestures at the impressive way they have hardly any space between them without actually touching.

I shake my head. "No. They're both quite oblivious to how they each feel toward each other because I don't think Young Jae's feelings are one-sided. They don't even tell us about it. They have such a close friendship, if Elise were to admit there are feelings, she would either have to end her friendship or her relationship, and I don't think she's ready to do either. And Young Jae is too good a man to do anything to upset Elise. So they remain friends, but the energy between them is palpable."

Adeline rests her chin on her palm, her eyes sad. "I get it. I don't know Jake, so I say this with my limited knowledge, but I hope those two find their way to each other. Elise doesn't look like that when she talks about Jake."

Looking over my shoulder, I watch as Young Jae heads toward the food, Elise turning and halting when she sees us both staring.

"What?" She flushes, coming to sit next to me.

"We were just admiring how good you two looked standing over there." Grinning, I lean toward her, murmuring, "Young Jae sure looks sexy in his suit, doesn't he?"

She smiles, her gaze dropping down to her hands as she nods. "He does."

Before we can say anything else, Owen and Cameron are at the table, setting down plates of food.

Cameron is easy to spot, he towers above everyone else and the buzzed head is a dead giveaway. Like Young Jae, he's dressed all in black except his mask. It looks like weathered iron, formed to look like something a warrior would wear. The sides are jagged edges angling up into points that reach up to his hairline. There's a simple but elegant notched design that I can't make out in the dark room.

Our eyes meet, my heart beating harder in my chest as Owen comes around to sit next to Adeline. Our group fades away, Cameron's hazel eyes are intense on me, and I can't look away.

They hold so much emotion, but what stands out to me is the hurt and the anger. That look fuels my own anger. He's the one that moved on in a minute. The dust from our breakup didn't even have time to settle before he found someone else. Shouldn't I be the one who is hurt and angry?

Jerking my head away, I look to where Owen has his arm draped over the back of Adeline's chair, whispering something private in her ear. They look so happy.

Out of the corner of my eye, I watch Cameron sit directly across from me, leaving the seat next to Elise empty. Our group is complete.

James is here somewhere, but he's likely sharing a table with the officers and their wives. Momentarily, I wonder if Caleb is around here too, but that look flies away when I glance back at Cameron, only to find him staring at me.

"We grabbed enough food for everyone, and Young Jae is coming back with a selection of desserts." Owen gestures to the smaller plates on the table and we all dig in.

Every time my eyes meet Cameron's, the tension between us thickens. It makes me wonder if we can even be friends or if this will never go away.

As we eat, I start to relax. The two glasses of wine don't hurt.

Elise and I regale Adeline with tales of past masquerade balls. There's always some drama that unfolds, usually harmless because tonight is the night the high school kids love to pull pranks.

"One year, we came outside, and all our vehicles had been plastic wrapped." Laughing, I take a sip of wine.

Adeline's eyes shine. "I wonder what they'll do tonight."

Everyone laughs. We've tried guessing before, but we've never gotten it right.

The music changes, Elise and I perking up as the K-pop

song she requested finally plays. We shove out of our chairs, pulling Adeline with us to the dance floor.

We're all a little buzzed, our inhibitions gone as we dance together. The dance floor is crowded, it always is, and the wide range of music that plays to accommodate everyone's tastes keeps people dancing all night long.

After a quick drink break, we're back on the floor. The buzz from earlier a little heavier, the excitement in the room heady.

The music changes to a slow song, Owen pulls Adeline into his arms. Smiling, I watch Young Jae offer his hand to Elise. Everyone is partnered up, and my heart twinges as I turn and start to make my way to the table. A hand on my arm stops me.

Turning, I inhale sharply when my eyes meet Cameron's. His gaze is intense as he pulls me into his arms, holding me close. The soft, masculine scent of his cologne assaults me. Memories of our past play in my mind as our eyes lock.

His hand imprints onto the skin on my exposed spine.

Wordlessly we dance. When it ends, I stop, but he doesn't let me go, and as the next song starts again, I follow his lead.

Dropping my chin, I stare at his chest as we dance, my heart racing. A shiver runs down my spine as I feel his breath on my ear. My entire body is on fire, my heart and my head warring with each other. The longing I've held onto fills me, but the hurt is also there, unwilling to let go of its grasp.

The song comes to an end. I feel his lips near my ear before I can say anything or look up at him.

"We have some things we need to talk about. I think I deserve some answers." Cameron's voice rumbles straight to my core, his words filling me with ice.

His arms fall away, leaving me chilled and stunned, watching Cam's back as he walks back to the table.

CHAPTER
Five

CAMERON

Flexing my hands, I turn away from the table and head outside to get some fresh air. Holding Rae in my arms again felt so right, but the hurt and confusion I've always held onto from our breakup came back in full force. Especially when I see my own feelings reflected in her eyes.

I need answers because that's the only way we can move forward, and I want to move forward with her. Holding her in my arms as we danced confirmed it for me, I want back what we had before life got so twisted.

A beer appears in front of me. Turning, I smile at Owen and Young Jae.

"Thought we'd find you out here." Young Jae looks at me empathetically. "I know it's hard now, but I think you and Rae could be friends eventually."

Clenching my jaw, I shake my head. "I don't want to be

friends. I want answers about what the hell happened five years ago. I'm here to fix the mistakes I made."

Answers I was too stunned and hurt to ask for at the time. And then I want to start from where we left off. I never should've let Rae go. I should've fought for her. I definitely shouldn't have married Sarah, she deserved better than that.

My head is cloudy as I take a deep drink of my beer. Everything about the situation could've and should've been handled differently, but now I have a chance to change how things go from here.

Owen looks thoughtful as we drink our beer in silence. "Are you ready to also give some answers?" His deep voice cuts into the air.

"What do you mean?" My voice comes out defensive. Smiling apologetically, I gesture for him to continue.

"I'm sure that Raelynn has questions for you as well. The hurt goes both ways. Are you ready for that?"

"I didn't end things with her." Crossing my arms, my eyes narrow.

He sighs, shaking his head. "No, you didn't. But you also didn't fight for her. And you had the dating apps downloaded how soon after she ended things? I'm sure to her it felt like a minute. Hurt goes in both directions, regardless of who ends things."

Tilting my beer back, I take a deep drink as his words turn around in my mind. I never really thought about how things appeared to Raelynn, regardless of whether it was true or not. Shame fills me and I drop down on the nearest bench. "I never thought about it." *Wow. That's pretty shitty of me.*

Young Jae sits down next to me. "This is exactly why

you need to join us on our annual retreat. Raelynn is coming, giving you plenty of time to talk to her. Get settled here first, think things through. Then, when we're out there, you can have your chat. You can even head out early if you need time to think away from town," Young Jae offers.

Glancing between my friends, I appreciate having them back in my life. I never really felt at home anywhere else. While I made friends and connections, most of them were through work or Sarah and they never felt as deep or meaningful as the friendships I left behind.

We finish off our beers and head back inside.

Our table is empty, so we go back to the dance floor. Owen looking for Adeline, a sweet woman I haven't really gotten to talk to much yet. Young Jae looking for Elise because those two are attached at the hip.

I can't keep myself away from Raelynn, not tonight. The Willowbrook Lake Annual Masquerade Ball is where we made our relationship official eighteen years ago. It's always held special meaning to us. The urge to be near her is too much to resist.

After some effort, we find the ladies dancing and totally smashed.

"Am I mistaken in that we were only gone for like twenty minutes tops?" Owen looks at us, his eyes wide.

Smirking, Young Jae shakes his head. "If that."

"To be fair, I'm pretty sure they were well on their way earlier," I mutter. We all chuckle.

Glancing at my watch, I can't believe that it's already past one in the morning. My eyes linger on Raelynn as she dances, narrowing when some dude crashes into her and she goes flying. Before she can hit the floor, I've caught her. "Watch it!" My tone is seething as I glare at the guy who rushes into the crowd away from me.

Raelynn giggles as I stand her upright, mumbling something I can't hear over the music. Looking over at the guys, I grit out, "I'm going to take her home."

They nod and I walk with her to the table so she can get her stuff. She's watching me, her dark brown eyes swirling with emotion as I pick up her purse. Taking her hand, I lead her out of the building, only stopping to pick her up when she stumbles.

"I'm fine. You're jus' walkin' too fast." Her voice has a slight slur.

I don't set her down. "I'm not letting you hurt yourself."

She mutters something under her breath, but I only catch the word "care."

Biting my tongue, I find my car and set her in the passenger seat. It's not until I pull out of the spot that I realize I don't have her current address. Stopping, I pick up my phone to text the guys, but they already beat me to it and sent me the info.

Raelynn's house is in one of the oldest neighborhoods in town. Her bungalow is in a corner lot backing onto the park that connects to the lake. It's cute and cozy, the massive yard swallowing the house. It's very different than what I expected because I know the house Raelynn has been dreaming about since childhood, a massive Victorian-style estate home. Despite that, I can see the appeal of the space.

Parking the car, I round the vehicle to open the door for

Rae. She sighs, taking the hand I've offered and steps gingerly out of the car. Her purse falls, so I bend to get it as Raelynn wavers on her feet.

Taking a deep breath, I close my eyes and prepare myself for what I know I have to do. Rae isn't typically a big drinker. Occasionally with the girls, but this is far past her usual tipsy limit.

Taking her hand, I guide her to the house. She takes her purse from me and finds her keys, fumbling to get it into the lock. Wrapping my hand around hers, I open the door and follow her inside.

A cream-colored blur comes racing up to us, purring as it wraps itself around Raelynn's ankles.

"Mocha!" Rae coos, bending down to scoop the cat up, making her stumble. Catching her by the hips, I grit my teeth as she slowly stands, still making baby talk at the cat. The cat who is staring at me over her shoulder. It's cute, the brown face and blue eyes grind into Rae's cheek, the purrs getting louder.

Bending down, I help her out of her shoes as she tries to kick them off. As soon as her feet are bare, she heads down the hall, a bit of steadiness returning. Removing my shoes without taking my eyes off her, I follow her into her kitchen where she's set Mocha onto the floor and is scooping her some food.

I dig around and find a glass, filling it with water before looking for some ibuprofen. Finding that too, I finally turn back to Raelynn. She's leaning on the counter, her beautiful brown eyes locked on me. They're glassy, but I can't tell if it's from the booze or tears.

Handing her the meds and the water, I watch as she drinks it.

She finishes it, her movements steadier as she puts the glass in the dishwasher.

"Thanks for driving me home." Her voice is quiet, the same distance in her tone that I felt five years ago when she told me she wanted to end things.

Nodding, I reply, "Yeah, no problem."

An awkward silence descends, so I say goodbye and turn to leave. Pausing as I glance into her living room, my eyes are drawn to a photo on her wall. I keep walking before she notices the direction I'm looking.

My footsteps are loud in the silence of the house. It only takes a short time to close the door behind me and get into my car, but my heart is pounding.

On her wall was a photo of us from one of our vacations. We're peeking our heads around a massive tree. Raelynn is smiling at the camera, but me—my eyes are on her.

CHAPTER
Six

RAELYNN

It's been two weeks since the masquerade ball. In that time, I've run into Cameron at least four times. Which is pretty surprising, even in our small town. Despite this, there's only been one occasion where we spoke to each other, and I was with a client so it was brief. Thank goodness.

I'm still trying to come to terms with the fact he's not only back but back permanently. What happened with him and Sarah? I heard they were married and then divorced within two months. That just doesn't seem like something Cameron would do. And then to come back after five years of being away. He didn't even come back to help his parents pack their house when they decided to move south.

Shaking my head, I shove these thoughts aside. It's

unlikely I will get any answers, and I have no right to them.

The bell at the front door of Perk Up jingles, and Adeline comes in looking frozen. It's just me and Elise in here, the frigid weather outside persuading people to stay home except for necessities.

Elise comes from where she was making lunch in the back, waving at Adeline who weaves through the dining area toward the table I've made into a workspace.

"Why is it so cold?" Adeline shrugs out of her coat. "I barely made it out of the driveway, even with Owen clearing it out."

"I don't know, but I hope it passes soon." I smother a yawn before gathering my papers and cleaning my mess off the table. "It makes business really slow. No one wants to look at houses when the air hurts your face. I hate not being busy, I need to find a hobby."

Adeline chuckles. "You're welcome to come my way any time. There's always an abundance of work that needs to be done around the acreage."

"Yeah, but you and Owen are in the honeymoon phase of a new relationship, and I don't want to interrupt."

Adeline rolls her eyes. "Don't be ridiculous. We're not teenagers."

The table is clear of my mess, and Elise brings out a plate of sandwiches and baked goods. "You could always start photography again. You have a talented eye when it comes to taking photos."

Humming, I nod. "It's true, I did enjoy taking photos and I have the time now. But I haven't really picked up a camera since my early twenties. I wonder if I remember how to use anything other than my phone camera anymore."

We gab around the table, laughing together. It's hard to believe Adeline has been here for less than six months, I already couldn't imagine not having her as a friend. She's kind and insightful, fun and joyful to be around.

"Adeline, are you coming to the winter retreat with us in January? I'm heading up a couple days early to clean up and have some quiet time. You're welcome to drive up with me." I lean back in my chair, hoping she agrees since I found out Cameron will be there too.

She nods. "Yeah, that's the plan, but unfortunately I can't head out early. I promised my parents I would head their way for New Year's."

Smacking my forehead, I mutter, "You told me that. I can't believe I forgot."

Adeline shrugs. "You've got a lot going on, I get it. It will be the first time I'm going that way since coming here and I really hope I don't run into Scott's mom."

Cringing, I recall what she told me happened at her husband's funeral. "I hope so too. Elise, do you want to head up early?"

"I'm sorry, I don't have coverage for here until the fifth," Elise says, her voice soft. "I will make up for it by prepping tons of yummy food to bring."

Disappointment fills me, but at least the house will be mine alone. Maybe I will bring my camera and take some photos. I miss tapping into my creative side and I think it would help ease some of my dissatisfaction with work.

Two hours later, I'm walking into my house, eager for some Mocha snuggles before searching for my camera. I like the idea of taking up photography again. It's something I enjoy doing, and having a creative outlet might help me deal with my dissatisfaction with work. Maybe I can offer to take some photos of Adeline and Owen.

Putting my shoes away, I call Mocha. Normally she greets me at the door, but sometimes she's late if she's sleeping or using the litterbox. My heart starts to race when she doesn't come. Rushing through the house, I find her in the kitchen making gagging noises. There are several spots where she's thrown up, a pinkish tinge in a couple of the spots.

Rushing to the closet, I grab her carrier, and we peel out of the driveway in less than five minutes. Mocha has never thrown up outside the random fur ball, and even those are rare.

Weaving through town, I come to a halt in the closest parking stall at Willowbrook Veterinary Clinic. Grabbing the carrier, I rush inside, my heart in my throat. There's no one in the waiting room, much to my relief, as I frantically ring the bell.

It's not until Cameron comes out of the back wearing a crisp white jacket that I remember Suzanne is only working at the clinic twice a week.

"Rae?" His eyes drop to the carrier and back to my tear-streaked face.

"Something is wrong with Mocha. She didn't greet me at the door, and when I went in the kitchen, she was gagging and surrounded by vomit." Choking the words out, I try to stop myself from sobbing. "Please help her. She's everything to me."

He gently takes my elbow, leading me into a clean

examination room. Without a word he gets to work checking her vitals and drawing blood. She meows in annoyance but still doesn't act like her usual active self.

"I know that hurts." Cameron coos at Mocha. "I promise I will take good care of you. Do you remember me from when I brought your drunk mama home?"

Mocha leans into him, totally sucking it up as Cam finishes his checks. He excuses himself, leaving me to fawn over Mocha.

"Shh, baby, whatever it takes, we will get you better." I kiss her head.

Cameron comes back in, an IV bag in hand. "She's a little dehydrated, so I'm going to get her started on some fluids while I run the remaining tests."

Chewing on my lower lip, I whisper, "Is she going to be okay?"

His hazel eyes meet mine, full of empathy and understanding. "From what I've seen, without having the test results, I think she has an infection. With a round of antibiotics, she should be just fine and back to her normal self within the next week."

Petting Mocha, I coo at her while he gets the IV set up and he leaves us to finish running the tests. The IV bag is nearly empty when he returns, his gaze apologetic.

"I'm sorry, I had another client I had to see." He unhooks the IV and leaves again, returning quickly with a syringe. "So, as I thought, she has an infection. I'm going to give her the first dose of antibiotics now. I will need you to bring her back at this time for the next four days for the rest. I want her on a specific dose, and it's just easier to monitor when given intravenously."

Slumping in relief, I nod. "Thank you, Cam."

He gives me some more instructions about care and things to watch for at home as I gently settle her back into the carrier. We walk out front together, and I pause at the desk. "How much—"

"Nothing. Just bring her back tomorrow."

When I open my mouth to argue, he lifts his hand, so I nod and thank him. I feel his eyes burning into my back as we leave, but I don't turn around.

I can't.

CHAPTER
Seven

CAMERON

Penelope comes to the back, her brows pinched together. "Dr. Hall, why is there a woman here saying her cat needs its daily antibiotic shot?"

Glancing at the time, I grin. "Because I told her she has to come here for the next four days so her cat can get the appropriate treatment."

She flips open the folder she's holding, the creases deepening. "We're not out of stock of the pills. I made sure of it."

Chuckling, I say, "I know. It's for personal reasons. You didn't happen to mention it's unusual, did you?"

Her brow smooths out, and she smirks. "I did not. I will put her in exam room two."

She goes out front, and I hear her voice carry through

to the back, asking Raelynn to go to the second exam room while I prep the antibiotic shot.

I enter the room almost immediately after Penelope returns to the front, checking out the patient I just finished with.

Raelynn doesn't notice me; she's cradling Mocha and talking to her in a loving voice. The cat is completely lapping it up, looking at her and slow blinking, a purr rumbling out of her so loud it doesn't seem to fit such a small critter.

"She looks much perkier today." I maintain my smile when Raelynn tenses.

She relaxes a bit as she turns to return my smile. "A little. No more vomit, and she greeted me at the door when I returned from running errands this morning. Still not quite her usual self, but way better than yesterday."

I take my time giving Mocha the shot. I spent all last evening thinking about all the things I need to say to Rae, but here isn't the place. I couldn't resist the excuse to talk to her, even for a few minutes. The temptation was enough to prompt her to come back.

"Are you going to Young Jae's cabin for the retreat?" I ask, but it's not really what I want to know.

"I am." She takes Mocha back into her arms, holding her close. "I heard you're coming too. It's always a lot of fun. The cabin is beautiful."

Young Jae designed and built the cabin three years ago and started his annual trip that winter. I've seen some of the pictures over the years, craving the ones that gave me a little glimpse into Rae's life.

"I'm looking forward to it."

Before I can say anything else, she jumps up and glances at the time. "I have an appointment in twenty, I better go." She pauses at the door, her eyes flitting to mine. "See you tomorrow, Cameron."

She's gone before I can respond, the soft scent of her perfume lingering in her wake.

The next day, we talked about work. And she stays a little longer than the day before.

On the third day, we discussed the changes to our friend group. The addition of Adeline.

Our group has always been solid and that didn't falter when Raelynn and I split, something that we didn't talk about, but she stayed for close to twenty minutes after Mocha got her shot.

The last day we talk about our families and what they've been up to. We skirt around the topic of how hard it was to lose those relationships after the split. I always enjoyed her family, so as she updates me on her parents and brother, I can't help but feel that twinge of nostalgia from being a part of her family.

This easy conversation is something I have missed these past five years. It feels like I'm reconnecting with my best friend, but there's the elephant in the room, which we will eventually need to address. I need to know why she decided to pull the plug on our relationship without bothering to give me a reason.

Almost as though Raelynn can tell where my thoughts are going, she stands and makes some excuse about needing to go. I let her, knowing that we would be having those conversations soon.

CHAPTER
Eight

RAELYNN

Checking the automatic feeder for the tenth time, I close it up and press the button to give Mocha a little treat. She's feeling better after her round of antibiotics, maybe a little smothered by me the past couple of weeks as I hovered to make sure she was back to normal.

Guilt weighs heavy on my chest that I'm leaving to go on a getaway so soon after she was ill, but the neighbor is going to check in on her daily and send me updates. I also brought her in for follow-up tests and everything came up normal.

Grabbing my bags, I run through my checklist once more before loading my truck. My suitcases, three coolers of food, plus all the dry goods. Since my vehicle is bigger, I offered to bring everything up for Young Jae. Grabbing my snowshoes and all my gear, it takes me close to twenty minutes to get everything loaded and my list triple checked.

The five-hour drive passes slowly taking close to six hours due to poor road conditions, the snow falling heavier as I turn onto the mountain road leading to the cabin. It's isolated, which is one of the reasons Young Jae bought the land. The scenery is beautiful, but it can be a tricky drive.

I'm moving forward at a snail's pace until I finally see the cabin through the trees. Slowing to a stop, I search my console for the garage door opener Young Jae gave me, pulling into the garage with a sigh.

By the time I'm done lugging everything into the cabin and putting it away, the snow is falling so hard that I can't see more than a couple feet in front of me. Staring out the window, I watch the peaceful scene.

Young Jae's cabin is located in a small valley. One of a few that are spaced several kilometers apart. It's surrounded by trees, and a small mountain lake is a short hike away.

Over the past few years, these trips have brought me peace and clarity. The snowcapped mountains seem to help me find whatever it is I need. The silence around me is different somehow from the silence at home. Oddly enough, I feel less lonely being here than surrounded by neighbors.

Closing my eyes, I take a deep breath, exhaling slowly. At least I have a couple days of this peace before it's disrupted by Cam's presence. Being near him when Mocha was sick brought all my feelings back to the surface. Not that they had far to come, but the love and hurt was all there, and I know being in close quarters with him here will mean dealing with them constantly bubbling beneath the surface.

Bundling up, I head out to the patio to gather some wood. I have a new book to read, but it wouldn't be as relaxing without the crackling of a good fire. Loading the carrier, I haul it into the house.

Rounding the corner into the living room, I see a figure looming at the window.

Screaming, I chuck the firewood at the intruder.

I charge at the person, panic making me forget the most important lesson of self-defense: get away.

Strong arms catch me, holding me firmly against a muscled chest.

"Raelynn, breathe. It's just me." Cameron's voice drains the adrenaline from my body and if it wasn't for the arms still holding me against his firm chest, I'd be on the floor.

He holds me, silent as I breathe through the haze of panic, letting me go when I'm coherent enough to process the racing of my heart due to his proximity and not fear.

Backing away, I close my eyes and take some deep breaths. Five years, and the effect he has on me hasn't diminished in the slightest. My mind is hurt, my body feels like it's home. I hate it.

Laughter cuts through the haze of attraction and regret. "What exactly were you trying to do?"

Crossing my arms, I meet his gaze with a scowl. "I was trying to shock you so I could overtake you."

He purses his lips, body vibrating, as he bends to gather the wood. "I was shocked, that's for sure."

"I'll have you know; I've done several self-defense

classes in the past five years. I could've at least contained you enough to escape."

He purses his lips, eyes dancing with laughter until I finally let out my own chuckle. The air thickens until I look away.

Cam sighs, turning toward the fireplace. "I'll get a fire going."

Watching as he cleans up and then starts building a fire, I listen to see if anyone else decided to come early, but all I hear are the sounds of our breathing and the lighting of a match.

"What are you doing here? I didn't think anyone was coming for a couple more days." Unable to stand the silence now that he's in the room, I try not to let my anxiety at being alone with him sour my tone. Dropping my arms, I walk to the couch and sit down, staring at my hands. This is the last thing I need right now. I still haven't sorted out all the things I want to say to him.

Or if I want to say anything at all, quite frankly.

The sound of burning wood fills the silence as he stands and turns toward me. "I decided to come up early and get a couple days of quiet."

He doesn't seem surprised to see me, but instead of asking him about it, I just nod slowly. "I see."

My eyes focus on the flames dancing over the wood as Cameron sits in the oversized armchair across from me. The silence is both familiar and uncomfortable. So many things unsaid between us.

The reality that Cameron is available and near has been taunting me since he got to town. The flicker of hope that I could never let go of has grown, but the hurt has also kept its hold. How can we move on from everything that happened after us? He found someone so immediately after we ended, that sense of betrayal and the feeling that our relationship was meaningless to him is one that I haven't been able to let go.

I'm sure he has things too that he wants to know, but it's hard for me to see past my own hurt.

Refusing to let him stop me from checking in with myself, I stand. Scoffing, I ignore the arch to his brows and turn to grab my book from my room.

It's going to be impossible to ignore that he's here, but this is one of my most anticipated getaways and I'm not going to allow Cam's sudden reappearance in my life to ruin it for me. We can hash it out later.

Returning with my book and a blanket, I settle onto the couch and dive in without a word.

I feel Cameron's gaze burning into me, but I continue to focus on the novel in my hands rather than the man who has haunted and starred in my dreams for as long as I've known him.

He finally stands up and goes into the kitchen. Breathing a sigh of relief, I flip back to the beginning of the novel and start over.

I'm fully engrossed in what I'm reading by the time Cam returns to the room, setting a cup of tea on the table next to me without a word before he settles back onto the armchair with his own book.

"Thank you, Cam." My voice is thick with emotion, so I don't look up. This reminds me of when we used to do this together regularly, except back then our legs would be tangled together. How does it feel like no time has passed while everything is completely different?

How can he feel so familiar and also like a complete stranger all at the same time?

Unable to handle those thoughts, I immerse myself into a fantasy world while I still can.

The day passes slowly, tension building in the room. It's impossible to pretend that Cam isn't sitting in the room across from me, his eyes burning into me even though I don't lift my eyes from the book in my hands.

The pages blur together after a while, my thoughts wandering through every possible scenario from the best to the worst.

By the time the sun sets, I decide to act like he's just another one of the friend group and ignore our history. At least until I can practice all the things I need to say.

Cam leaves the room with a sigh, bustling about the kitchen. Closing my eyes, I pinch the bridge of my nose and close my book.

"You can do this. For the sake of your heart and our social group, woman up." Muttering to myself, I put my book away and join Cam in the kitchen.

His back is to me, a knife moving deftly over some veggies.

"Can I help?" My voice is strong despite the emotional rollercoaster.

Cam stills, his fingers flexing before he turns to me. "Sure. Could you prep the pan for the chicken stew? And make some of your dinner rolls? They always go so well with stew."

Joining him in the kitchen, we work around each other,

silently putting together dinner. Handing him the pan I've prepped, I move on to mixing the dough for buns.

Everything flows seamlessly as we fall into a pattern that my muscles still remember. After we broke up and I had the chance to reflect, I realized I'd shut him out in our journey to have a baby to protect him to my own detriment, and that decision was what ultimately broke me down to the point I couldn't continue on. It was the wrong thing to do, but by the time I realized my mistake and wanted to fix it, he had already met Sarah.

Things might have been different if he hadn't jumped into the dating pool what felt like minutes after we ended.

Closing my eyes as he brushes past me, I finish rolling out the buns, pop them into the oven, and set my timer.

Somehow, despite the silence, the air feels less tense. I move to the sink and start washing dishes, handing them off to Cameron until everything is done and the kitchen is clean.

Cam checks the stew. "It should be ready in about fifteen minutes. I will go grab some wood for the fire. Did you want to open a bottle of wine?"

Nodding, I watch him head out before grabbing the wine and popping the cork. Dinner with Cam and a bottle of wine, what could go wrong?

CHAPTER
Nine

CAMERON

With the fire crackling, I head back to the kitchen to find two glasses of red wine on the island and Rae pulling the fresh buns out of the oven. She works quickly to spoon the stew into bowls, her expression carefully neutral as she works.

The way we fell so quickly into the rhythm of our past felt so natural, but I miss the gentle touches and easy conversation that used to flow. I guess not everything comes back quite so effortlessly.

Taking the dish offered to me, I grab my glass of wine and sit at the table. Raelynn sits across from me, her eyes low as she sips at her drink before serving up some food.

After eating in silence for a few minutes, I can't take it anymore. I may not want to delve into everything I need to get off my chest, but this silence is killing me.

"How's work been?" It's lame, the way two strangers or new acquaintances might converse, but it's a start.

She takes a sip of her wine and shrugs. "It's fine. I think it's time for something new. I just don't enjoy it the same way I once did. Elise suggested exploring graphic design again, but I haven't really done anything other than think about making a change. In the meantime, I'm attempting to get back to photography to fill my cup."

I think about how much she used to love art, her creative eye impeccable. "When did you stop taking photos?"

Her expression turns sad, but when she replies her tone is casual. "Five years ago. I picked up a lot of work, including around some of the neighboring towns, and didn't have time."

Brows pinching together, I feel more confused than before. She doesn't make eye contact as she finishes her glass of wine, her focus turning to her food as she falls silent and eats the rest of her stew.

"I hope you find time to pick it up again. You have real talent." It hurts to think she hasn't taken the time to do something she loves for so long, but I'm also confused about everything. I don't understand why she ended our relationship and then seems so hurt by it that she would abandon doing something she loves. Nothing makes any sense.

"I brought my camera with me. Tomorrow I'm going to head out early to try and get some good shots in." She pours another glass and drinks almost the entire thing in one go.

"I'm glad." When she doesn't say anything, I get up and start clearing the table and cleaning up. From the corner of my eye, I see her top her glass up again.

"How are things at the clinic?" The slight edge to her tone is gone, and the warmth in its place is a direct result of the wine she's polished off. It takes me back to the shared dinners in our small apartment kitchen.

Being back in Willowbrook Lake, seeing Raelynn, it all makes me realize how much I've missed and how much I regret letting her go without a fight.

"It feels like coming home. The clientele has transitioned better than expected, so Suzanne will begin phasing out sooner than we thought. I would guess as soon as I'm back from the cabin rather than another six months. Penelope is amazing. The way she organizes things made the transition simple." Returning to the table, I pour myself another glass of wine, emptying the bottle. "Why don't we go sit in the living room?"

Rae nods. I stand back, letting her lead the way. Her hips sway, drawing my eyes down. My body immediately reacts to the way her leggings mold to the shape of her ass. Thankfully I'm still wearing jeans from earlier, so the hard-on I'm sporting is only marginally noticeable.

When she sits on the loveseat, I grin and plop down on the opposite end. She swallows hard but doesn't move away.

"What about the other staff? How have they adjusted?" She sips at her wine, setting the glass down and tucking her knees to her chest.

"Good. The vet tech, Ashton, is really good. He's very

competent and we've found a good flow. Rita, the groomer, is quiet, but she's good with the animals and basically does her own thing. Suzanne set it up quite well by renting her the grooming space at a discounted cost and Rita helps with any patients as needed."

We talk until the fire burns down to embers, and even though we never touch on our past, it feels good to have a normal conversation with her. I don't know where her head is at, but right now I'm happy to pretend everything between us is okay, just for the night.

"I think I'm going to get some water. Would you like some?" she asks.

"That would be great, thanks."

Rae leans to grab my glass from the table at the same time I do, our hands brushing, heads close.

Her breath catches as she pulls her hand back, her eyes locking on mine. Our faces are inches apart, her cheeks flushed. The air thickens between us as we stare, the tension pulsing.

She tracks my tongue as I lick my lower lip. Unable to stop myself, I reach my hand out to tuck an errant strand of hair behind her ear, groaning when she closes her eyes, leaning into it.

Before I can stop myself, my lips are on hers. Beyond the hint of wine, she tastes the same.

Rae moans, closing the distance between us as she wraps her arms around my neck. Deepening the kiss, I pull her onto my lap, letting her control the pace of the kiss. She grinds her hips into me, molding herself as close as she can.

Holding her to me, I stand and stride to my room, pausing outside the door.

Rae lifts her head in question.

My heart pounds at the thought of stopping this, but I can't help but think about how she ran from me and never looked back. Rae has been the woman of my dreams since I first saw her. As much as I want this, I need to know this isn't some mistake she's going to regret.

"Are you sure?" I don't want her to change her mind. I need to see if what I'm feeling is anywhere close to what she is, but I refuse to let this be another wedge.

"Yes." Her voice is throaty, eyes dilated as she grinds her hips, the heat of her core pressing against my erection.

"Good."

Kicking the door open, I set her on the bed. Before I can do anything, her shirt is on the floor, the rest of her clothes quickly joining them as I devour seeing her for the first time in too long. Her brown skin is as smooth as I remember and begging for my hands. She always did have the softest skin.

Rae makes an impatient noise as she inches up the bed. Smirking, I strip slowly, finally stroking my cock as she licks her lips. Her eyes leave a hot trail as they make their way down.

Crawling over her, I capture her lips, teasing her with the tip of my cock, but pull away when she arches into me.

Kissing along her jaw and down her neck, I circle my tongue around one of her nipples, cupping the other breast in my hand. Her body is all soft skin and curves as I explore with my hands, lips, and tongue.

Her whimpers and moans as I make my way down to

her sex has my cock pulsing. It's so hard, it's almost painful, but I refuse to take her without tasting her first.

Teasing her with the softest touch of my finger, I groan at how wet she is, and all my self-control breaks. Delving my tongue into her sweet heat, I savor her as her hips buck into my face, her hands gripping the sheets.

Slipping two fingers inside, I curve them as I suck her clit, her pussy pulsing around me as she comes. My lips quirk, pleased knowing I can still make her come so quickly.

Before she can say anything, I move my way up her body, positioning myself between her legs, when I pause.

"Shit. No condom."

"I'm on the pill," she chokes out, lifting her hips.

Closing my eyes, I thrust into her, hard.

She cries out in pleasure, her hips meeting mine as I move. She feels incredible, her pussy clenching around me as we move.

Somehow, even after all this time, it feels right. And when I look down at Rae, her eyes on mine, I can see she feels the same. In the depths of her deep brown eyes, I can see the love she has for me despite everything, the emotion making them glisten with so many unsaid words.

She closes her eyes as she cries out, an orgasm tensing her entire body.

Dropping down to kiss her as I come, I soak in the warmth of her embrace as we still, lying in each other's arms.

Too quickly, she squirms from under me, racing to the adjoining bathroom where I hear water running. She comes back, sliding under the covers and lying on her side to look at me.

We don't say anything, knowing in this moment we need no words. I just don't know what tomorrow will bring.

CHAPTER
Ten

RAELYNN

Cam's soft breathing is everything I've missed at night for the past five years, yet sleep eludes me. My head is spinning a heady cocktail of post-sex bliss and confusion over where this takes us. One evening alone and we end up in bed. I don't regret what happened. It was amazing, and god, I missed him, but what does it mean? We can't simply move past everything that lingers unsaid. What if, after all that, we realize there's no coming back, that the hurt is too much?

Was this a potential goodbye?

My heart can't take that. Ending our relationship is my single greatest regret, something that tortures me every damn day. To have this chance and lose it, I would never be the same.

His phone beeps, the light bright in the dark room.

Doubt fills my mind. Who could possibly be messaging him at this hour? He's single again, and if history is an indication, he could already be on dating apps again.

Not that I have any right to wonder, but the idea sits sour in my stomach. The light quickly fades and I attempt to fall back asleep, but I lie there until the early morning light appears around the edges of the curtains.

I slide out of bed and tiptoe out the door to my room. I quickly change, bundling up and digging out my snow-shoes, before grabbing my camera and heading out the door.

The freezing air hits like a ton of bricks, leaving me breathless as I pull my scarf a little higher and start heading to my favorite photo spot. There's a little alcove that's sheltered from the elements that provides an incred-ible view of a small mountain stream that rarely freezes. The constant flow of water attracts animals for perfect photo opportunities.

The hike takes me about forty-five minutes. As the sun continues to rise, I wonder if Cameron has woken up yet. He likely won't be happy I'm gone, but I need this time to formulate how to have the conversation with him. Besides, I did tell him I was planning on taking photos this morning.

Our friends will arrive tomorrow, so it's today or not until we're home. And if last night was any indication, sooner would be better. I could see all the same emotions that swirled through me reflected in his eyes.

My stomach clenches when I think about all the ways the conversation can go wrong. After all these years, it's hard for me to imagine there's anything we can say that will get us past the hurt. I'm not innocent by any means. I am the one who ended it, but his actions afterward left a searing scar on me that I don't know how to move on from.

Settling into the alcove, I change the lens on my camera so I can see the stream. It's about seventy-five feet away, which is perfect for keeping a safe distance. The animals typically come out of an adjacent valley to the stream before working their way along one of the many trails.

Adjusting my bag so my bear spray is accessible, I settle in.

After close to thirty minutes of sitting, I tilt my neck to stretch, groaning as it cracks. The air has warmed slightly, but it's still freezing. I'm about to reach for my mitten warmers when a movement by the stream catches my eye.

Lifting my camera, I gasp when I spot a lynx. It crouches down by the water, drinking.

Adjusting the lens, I snap a ton of photos before it slinks back into the trees. Slumping against the rock, I cradle my camera to my chest in wonder. I thought maybe I would see a deer. Possibly an elk.

Never in my wildest dreams did I think I would see the elusive lynx.

Maybe today will be okay.

———

Reaching the top of the ridge, the cabin comes into view, smoke billowing from the chimney. I breathe a sigh of relief. The hike back always feels longer than the hike to the alcove, and some fresh snow has covered my tracks from this morning.

As I close the distance between me and Cameron, the things I need to say swirl through my head, a loud rumbling fills the air, and the ground starts vibrating slightly. Glancing around, I don't see anything but rush to get inside, tripping on my snowshoes. That sound only means one thing: avalanche.

The noise and vibrations are quieter in the house. Checking my phone, the Wi-Fi is down. Shit.

Cameron enters the living room when the door bangs shut behind me, his expression relieved when he sees me.

"I'm pretty sure that was an avalanche. The power is out." He huffs out a sigh. "If it was in the pass, no one is coming in or out, potentially for days."

Licking my lips, heat courses through me when his eyes drop to follow the path of my tongue. I let out a heavy sigh. "At least we're fully stocked."

He nods, leaving to grab more firewood while I unbundle and wrap my head around being potentially trapped with Cameron for who knows how long.

CHAPTER
Eleven

CAMERON

The sound of a door closing wakes me. The dim morning light peeks around the corners. I don't need to roll over to know that Raelynn is gone. Being with her, it was everything I've been missing.

Rubbing my hands over my face, I sigh. I don't know what I expected, but waking up alone after an incredible night was not on the list. She did say she was going to take photos. I just figured maybe we would eat breakfast first. Maybe I need to prepare myself to be shot down, but I saw the way she looked at me, and I don't think she's let go of her feelings.

Now, we just need to figure out how to work through the issues and see where it takes us. I can't let her go again without at least clearing the air. If she still doesn't want to be together after that, I will force my heart to move on.

Grabbing my phone, I see a message came through late last night.

Opening the app, my brows pinch together when I see Sarah's name.

> Hey, Cam. The sale of the house fell through. Something came up in the financing. It's listed again and I will keep you posted. I hope you're doing well. I know that being back in your hometown is a lot. I'm here for you if you need me.

Rubbing a hand over my hair, I gaze at the words on the screen. I've known her for five years and spent the past two years in a relationship with her. Her kind words remind me why we moved from friends to more, even if it was misguided. Her kind heart is one of her best qualities.

Licking my lips, I type out a response.

> Thanks for taking care of this. I'm sorry you have to do it on your own. I appreciate the offer. I'm doing okay so far.

Hitting send, I read it over, not really sure how I feel about my reply. Sarah helped me through the worst time of my life, conversation always flowing easily. I know my reply is stilted, but I don't want to complicate things more than they already are.

When she doesn't respond, I plug my phone in and move toward the window. Raelynn will likely be gone for a couple hours, giving me time to articulate everything I need to say. The entire house is silent. I've been in the city too long. The complete quiet is a little unnerving. Willowbrook Lake is muted compared to the city, but there's still the faint sounds of life around town.

Out here, there's nothing. Maybe the odd sound from the house, but Young Jae did an amazing design job, mitigating most of it. Leaving me with nothing to keep me occupied but my thoughts.

Rolling out of bed, I clean up the mess of my clothes from the night before, tossing them into the laundry bag I brought before throwing on my gray sweats and a T-shirt.

A rumbling sound filters into the house, and some pictures on the wall vibrate.

"What the fuck?"

Grabbing my phone, I go to message Young Jae, but the Wi-Fi is down.

I hear the front door close with a bang. Breathing a sigh of relief, I join Rae in the living room. She's bundled up, looking a little shaken.

I've felt this before, snowboarding down a mountain and seeing an avalanche in a nearby valley.

After letting her know about the avalanche theory, I head outside to gather some firewood. If the pass is covered, it gives me more time to figure things out with Raelynn. Despite the predicament of no power, I don't mind being trapped here with her.

———

The fire crackles as the light from the day fades. Raelynn and I spent most of the day rearranging the living room to accommodate both of us staying in there close to the heat from the fire while the power is out. In spite of Rae's best efforts, the area we were able to clear for sleeping is intimate.

Covering a smile as she eyes the loveseat, I see the moment she resigns herself to the fact it's not going to work for her to sleep on. While there's a lot of seating in the room, Young Jae opted for loveseats and cozy chairs versus a large couch.

The room is charged as we settle into chairs close to the fire. Aside from talking about how we want to manage food and the cold until the power comes back on, we haven't spoken much. Now that the work is done, last night looms between us.

Rae glances at me, dropping her gaze when her eyes meet mine. She nibbles on her bottom lip and clears her throat.

"I'm going to grab a snack for us." She leaves the room without giving me time to respond.

I want to talk to her about the end of our relationship, but the question is, where do I even start?

She comes back holding a plate with sandwiches and a couple bottles of water.

Biting back a grin, I ask, "No wine today?"

Her lips twitch in response. "No, I think we need to keep our wits about us because we have to watch the fire."

Thanking her when she hands me a sandwich and water, we sit quietly as we eat, both consumed by our thoughts.

Raelynn brushes her hair out of her face, shaking her head.

Finishing my food, I take a sip of water and a deep breath. "We should talk about last night."

She swallows, remembering the way it felt to be together. Heat fills the space between us, tension building as her eyes meet mine. I ponder kissing her again, knowing where it would lead, but I hold myself back until she nods, rubbing the palms of her hands over her pants.

Clearing my throat, my voice is low as I say, "It was— incredible. And I have no regrets, but there is so much I need to say."

She sets her empty plate down. Her voice is soft as she chooses her words carefully. "It was amazing. And I also don't regret it. It took me back to—the way things were."

Something about that hits a nerve. The warmth I feel floods away, leaving me cold as I snap, "The way things were. They could've stayed that way, but you decided to give up on us. To stop caring and trying. It was so easy for you. Was last night just a way to scratch an itch or—"

Her head jerks back, hurt, and then anger crosses her face. She doesn't let me finish as she leans forward, her entire body practically vibrating with emotion.

CHAPTER
Twelve

RAELYNN

His words are like a slap across the face, regardless of the hurt and truth behind them. I did give up on us, but to say I'm scratching an itch, I can't even believe he would think that.

"Fuck you, Cameron. Fuck you." My body shakes, I'm so angry. He grimaces when I point at him and lean forward, my voice low and hard. "Ending things with you is my single greatest regret. One I have attempted to deal with every single day for five years. I was on anti-depressants for two years after we broke up."

Taking a breath, I hold my hand up when he attempts to speak. "But this isn't all on me. I was dealing with so much more than I realized, and I needed you to say, 'I see you and I'm here for you.' Not recluse yourself into whatever project you had on the go or the newest game that caught your attention."

He jumps in, his brows furrowed, lips pressed thin. "I was there for you. I held you every time the test said negative. I tried to stay positive when it seemed hopeless."

Sighing, I shake my head. "I think you tried, in your way. I couldn't see it because I didn't hear the words. I needed the words. It wasn't until I was on my own that I fully processed that. Someone to help guide me through the struggles as we faced countless negative pregnancy tests and the emotional toll that took on me. That person should've been you. Instead, I couldn't tell you how much I was hurting because it felt like you couldn't handle it. Yes, you held me, but I couldn't handle the anguish on your face every time. And as we went, the comfort reduced, and you buried yourself in other things. So I tried to protect you by keeping it to myself."

"I didn't ask you to protect me!" he yells.

Standing, I cross my arms. "You didn't have to. You shut down every damn time. You would hug me, pat my back, and then retreat as rapidly as you possibly could."

"Then you should've told me how you were feeling. How the hell was I supposed to know?" His tone lowers, his body tense.

Throwing my arms out, I scream, "I couldn't fucking tell you. I shouldn't have had to tell you that I needed you for more than a cursory comfort. We stopped doing anything together that remotely resembled caring for our relationship until I quit showing you how much I was hurting. But it was too much trying to shield you and deal with the pain, so I ended it."

He huffs, pinching the bridge of his nose. "It was so easy for you to end things, like our life together, the time we had, didn't even matter."

"How can you possibly say that to me? After I told you how much I regretted it? I have been haunted by you for the last five years, completely heartbroken at the irreparable damage I did." Shaking my head, I run my hand over my eyes, the tension building. "And talk about hypocrisy. How long did it take you to move on? A minute? You think it was easy for me? Hearing about you appearing on dating apps. Seeing you move on so damn fast from the time you moved away to when you met Sarah. What was it, like a month? How dare you tell me this was easy for me."

My voice is hoarse, thick with emotion and all the pent-up feelings I'm finally releasing. My soul is raw as I lay myself bare.

He holds my gaze, emotions flitting over his face as he processes.

I watch as he closes his eyes and pinches the bridge of his nose. "I think we need to clear the air on that."

When he opens his eyes to look at me, I give a sharp nod, not trusting my voice.

"Shortly after we broke up, I went out for drinks with some buddies from college. I had been sulking and they took me out to play pool. Drinks were flowing and toward the end of the evening, they were going on about online dating. I signed up to get them to shut up, not intending to do anything with it." He locks eyes with me, all the hurt and the love and the intensity of everything clear on his face. "While I was playing pool, one of the guys grabbed my phone. I was pretty out of it, so I didn't think much of it."

Air whooshes out of me as he pauses. "You may have signed up because of pressure from your friends, but you still moved on in the blink of an eye."

"No, I didn't. In the morning, I received a message from the app. My friend had matched me with someone and set up a date for that day. It was Sarah, confirming the date in an hour. I went, only to explain what happened so I didn't leave her hanging. I figured the least I could do was explain and buy her a coffee." He stands up, closing a bit of the distance between us. "We got along really well, but we only talked as friends. Rae, I didn't start dating Sarah until two years ago when our friendship transitioned into more. After a year, I proposed. It felt like the next step for where we were at in our lives. Then we got married. It didn't take long to realize we made a mistake. We should've stayed friends, but we were comfortable together and mistook the friendship and comfort to be something it wasn't. Dating was the last thing on my radar after our relationship ended. I was too heartbroken."

He's sincere as he speaks and I know he's being honest. It's how Cameron is.

A weight lifts off my heart, knowing that he didn't move on immediately after we ended. A scoff huffs out. I can't believe I've been torturing myself for years over something that wasn't even true.

My knees start to shake, but I force myself to stay standing. My voice quivers. "I realized I made a colossal mistake not long after, but by then, Sarah started showing up in your posts on social media. You seemed so happy in a way that was painful to watch until I couldn't bear it, so I deleted you from my social media accounts. I couldn't bear to see you move on when I had made such a horrid mistake."

"I wish you would've had faith in me, in our relationship, to have a frank discussion with me. I don't need to be protected from how you feel, Raelynn. You should've talked to me." Cameron rests his elbows on his knees, leaning toward me, his gaze intense.

Taking a deep breath, I nod. "I know. Even after, I wish I would've said something to at least ease my heart, but my pride got in the way."

We fall silent, the revelations both freeing and heartbreaking.

But then…

"It hurts knowing that you were with Sarah for a year and asked her to marry you when we were together for a decade, trying for a baby, and you never asked me." My voice is soft, and telling him this is hard. Really damn hard. "Why was she enough to marry and I wasn't?"

It's hard to hold his gaze, but I need his answer. When I thought he proposed after four years, it hurt, but to find out he proposed after one hurts even more.

Sadness and regret flash across his face. He closes the distance between us, lifting his hands to rest on my shoulders. "You were more than enough. I wanted to propose to you, but when we were in school and getting started, it didn't feel like the right time, and then we started trying to get pregnant. With every disappointment, it felt like if I proposed, the moment would be overshadowed by the ghost of the baby we wanted so badly. Then we were over." He pauses, thinking through his next words carefully. "I don't have a good answer to why I proposed to Sarah after a year. We were in a comfortable place, and like I said, it seemed like the next step. I've spent the past five years trying to be happy, and as much as Sarah and I should've just stayed friends, she played a big role in helping me move on with my life. It was easy to confuse those feelings because I missed that belonging of having someone to come home to."

Taking a shaky breath, I pull away as I try to process the information overload. My body feels heavy. The emotion dump I released, followed by Cam's revelations, is too much. We lost so much time together, held back by my own stubbornness.

The past five years have been tainted by the actions I haven't been able to forgive myself for. Don't get me wrong, I've been happy overall, but the hindsight of my relationship with Cam has haunted me, and it was all for nothing.

Looking up at the ceiling, I will the burning behind my eyes to go away before I meet Cam's gaze. He's intense, those hazel eyes seeing too much.

The air thickens, our emotions laid bare.

With a growl, Cam prowls over to me, never dropping my gaze as he falls to his knees and pulls me into his arms. Lips crashing onto mine, I melt into him.

He grabs my hips, pulling me on top of him as he falls back onto the makeshift bed. Everything we've been carrying pours out of us as we kiss. Sitting up, I pull my shirt off, my bra quickly following. Cam groans as I kiss him again, pressing my body into his.

He flips me onto my back, pulling his shirt over his head before meeting my lips again.

Last night, we were a little tipsy, and everything was hurried, intense, and full of repressed feelings.

This time feels different, less hurried. We poured so much out, and the revelations tonight make my heart yearn for what we lost. A little crack appears in the shield I hold close to myself. I don't know where we go from here, but as Cam's hands work his magic, I feel a flicker of hope.

CHAPTER
Thirteen

RAELYNN

I wake up alone in front of the fire, my body aching deliciously from last night. Yawning, I pull the covers up to my chin, snuggling in. The heavy weight I've been carrying on my chest has eased and after falling asleep in Cameron's arms last night, the hope flickering from last night has exploded into a full on flame. We can move past this, work through the past and the hurt, and get back what we had.

I'm not naïve enough to think it's going to be easy, but if we both want it, then there's hope we can come through.

A gust of cold air blows in as the door swings open, Cam kicking it shut behind him as he sets down a new load of wood.

"Power is still out, but hopefully, they will get that up

today even if they can't clear the pass yet." He shrugs out of his jacket, bringing the wood to pile next to the fireplace.

Sitting up, I hold the blanket to me and nod. "They're usually on top of these things."

We're quiet. Shifting in place, I stand, keeping the blanket wrapped around me. "I'm, ah, going to go get dressed."

Shuffling out of the room, I feel Cam's eyes burning into my back.

My room is freezing cold, so I don't waste any time getting dressed and heading back into the warm radius of the flames that Cam has stoked. He has a camping kettle hanging from a hook and a mixture of finger foods waiting on a plate.

Sitting next to him, I grab an apple slice and munch on it, my mind swirling with incoherent thoughts. I've always prided myself in being articulate and strong, but something about this situation with Cam has stripped me bare of that.

Finally, I just ask the question I can't keep out of my head. "What are we doing? Where is this going?"

He adjusts himself to face me directly, his eyes searching mine. "I would like to think we're finally addressing things and moving forward. I haven't stopped thinking about you for even a single day. And we have our chance now to work through everything and see where it takes us. I don't have an answer about where we're going. I think we both need to work through things together as well as on our own. There are things I know I've never dealt with and I believe you're in the same boat. So let's work on ourselves, and let's work on us. Then we can decide where it's going."

"I don't know if I can just be friends with you." I've known that truth even when I told myself we could, but it's not possible for me to separate myself from how I feel.

"We can just take it one day at a time. Let's not label it yet, because it would be too easy for me to say let's jump all in, and I don't think that would be good for either of us." His voice is gentle, and even though I want to just jump in, I know we need to take things slow.

"Okay. One day at a time."

The kettle whistles, and Cam fills two mugs that he's already scooped some hot chocolate into. He mixes one, handing it to me before finishing his own.

As we sip, I try to think of things we can do while being limited to one warm room when some board games catch my eye, one in particular, Rummikub.

Jumping up, I grab the box. "Ohmigod. Do you remember playing this when we were broke twenty-year-olds?"

He sees the game and bursts out laughing. "Remember? What I remember is having to pick all the pieces off the floor when I was kicking your ass, and your sweater 'accidentally' knocked them off."

Scowling, my lips twitch. "It was an accident. Besides, I was about to win."

Shaking his head, he clears the bed out of the way, moving the coffee table next to the fire. "Wanna bet?"

Sitting on the other side of the table, I start setting up the game. "What are the terms?"

"You win, and we do an activity of your choosing. I

win, and I get to choose." His smile turns wicked, and my stomach flips as I consider all the possibilities.

Agreeing, we dive in. I'm rusty in the game but determined to prove I can win. Throughout the game we tease each other, just like when we were first living together. Things are easy and we laugh a lot.

Cam pulls ahead almost immediately, laying tiles nearly every round.

"Oh, I told you I am the master." His tone is teasing as he lays down more tiles. Next round and I'm pretty sure he could win.

Taking a deep breath, I stare intently at the three rows of tiles before me. My last couple of rounds have not gone well but as I look, I grin.

Laying out tile after tile until the last one is placed, I yell, "I win!"

Cam stares down, shaking his head in bewilderment before swiping the tiles off the table and laying over it until he is inches from my face. "So, winner, what activity will you choose for us."

Chewing my lower lip as I ponder, his nearness sets me on fire. Smirking, I lean in a little until our noses are almost touching. "I know just the thing."

CHAPTER
Fourteen

RAELYNN

A snowball comes flying past my head as I dodge and throw a reciprocating snowball at Cam. He tucks and rolls, getting stuck in the snow.

I take advantage of the situation, lobbing another snowball at him and hitting him on the side of the head.

"Holy shit, that's cold." He chatters when the snowball goes down the back of his jacket.

"Oops." I giggle, turning to run when he charges after me.

Despite the two feet of powder, he easily catches me and tackles me to the ground. "I thought we said no head shots?" His voice is a growl, but I can hear the laughter behind the words.

"Bad aim." Squirming, I try to wriggle out from under

him, but he rolls me over, pinning me down. The snow is so deep that I sink down in my effort to escape.

Hazel eyes twinkle at me as he tucks an errant curl under my hat. "Broken rules mean consequences. How should I punish you?"

He leans down, his lips getting closer to mine. My breathing shifts as I lick my lips when he sits up throwing handfuls of snow into the air that fall over us.

Laughing, we wrestle until we're both covered, our cheeks tingling from the cool air.

I drop onto my back, moving my arms and legs back and forth. Cam watches momentarily before falling back into the snow and doing the same.

We used to play outside on snowy days like this all the time, so when I won the game, I knew I wanted to continue to revisit happy memories.

I still, looking over at him. "I missed this."

"I did too."

We lay there for a while, silently, until he stands carefully not to ruin his snow angel. He helps me up and we admire our masterpieces. Side by side, two perfect imprints.

The wind picks up, biting at my cheeks.

"I vote for hot chocolate and another round of Rummikub." Teeth chattering, I adjust my coat and turn toward the cabin.

Cam dashes past me. "Last one inside goes last."

"Cheater!" I take off after him, scooping more snow, forming a ball, and letting it fly. It hits him square in the back, stunning him, so I can run past, barely making it in the door before he does.

Stumbling into the house, I kick my winter gear off before noticing the entryway is warm. Flicking the light switch, I cheer when the light comes on.

"We have power again!" Spinning, I frown when Cam looks less thrilled. "What's wrong?"

He hangs up his winter gear, before pulling me into his arms. "I dunno, I guess I liked our cozy sleeping situation and our bubble. But you're right, it's good news. That means the road to here will be clear soon, so the house will fill up."

Hugging him back, I tilt my head to look up at him. "It's been nice, but we knew this would end. Now we need to figure out how to exist in reality as we navigate whatever happens between us."

He nods, squeezing me gently before he lets me go.

Together we put the living room back to rights, the house slowly warming up as the furnace works overtime to catch up.

"I have to commend Young Jae on the design of this house. It's a testament to the thought he put into how it was built that the pipes didn't freeze," Cam comments as he starts on dinner.

Joining him in the kitchen, we fall into the same sync we had the first night, but this time, conversation flows and instead of jumping away when we brush against each other, there are teasing comments and knowing glances.

As I lay in my bed, thinking about our day, I miss having him next to me, but we have no idea when our friends will be joining us and I know I'm not ready to fully involve them. We need to keep working on things, but around our friends I want to take it slow. Just in case.

CHAPTER
Fifteen

CAMERON

The door bursts open as Rae and I play another round of Rummikub, our friends piling in with their bags. They all stop when they see us, looks ranging from surprise, to relief, to pure smugness.

We stand, helping them bring their stuff in as they all talk about the avalanche.

"We finally made it! Quite a few powerlines went down, and the road took a long time to clear." Young Jae smiles, his face clearing of some of the stress he's been carrying.

"How did you pass the time? It must have been freezing in here." Owen's lips twitch, his tone suggestive. Adeline, who I met at the masquerade ball, elbows him in the ribs.

Laughing, I gesture to the coffee table. "A lot of Rummikub by the fire."

"I'm pretty sure the last time you two played that game, the pieces ended up on the floor along with"—Elise covers Young Jae's mouth with her hand before he can finish his sentence. He keeps going, muffled through her hand—"most of your clothes."

She glances at me before looking at Rae. "Why don't we get settled, and then we can all play? I brought pizza that is ready to go in the oven."

Rae follows her to the kitchen, getting the oven going before they head to one of the bedrooms. Adeline comes out of the room she and Owen will share, looking a little flushed and racing after them.

The guys are on me as soon as Elise's door closes.

"Well, looks like you didn't kill each other, so that's a good sign," Owen quips.

"I figured you would have an extra night, not several. I hope you made good use of your time." Young Jae drops onto the loveseat, his fingers tapping the armrest.

My lips twitch, but I don't bother to stop the grin. "Honestly, it was better than expected once the awkwardness passed. We will see where it goes, but I feel optimistic that coming back wasn't a mistake."

They look relieved and happy.

"I can't lie, I was a bit worried, but I'm glad to see you looking happy." Owen claps his hand on my shoulder before resetting the game.

The women join us, all smiles as they sit around the table. We start selecting our tiles as I remind them of the rules.

We dive into a game, eating pizza and chatting about everything that's been happening in their lives.

As we play, I feel happier than I have felt in five years. I missed my friends, spending time with them as we laugh and joke.

Adeline is the perfect addition to our group and I've never seen Owen smile more than he does with her. She softens him in a way I never thought possible.

"Okay, I give up. I can't win this game." Young Jae holds his hands up, laughing. "I'm going to get the hot tub going if anyone wants to join me."

We all agree that the hot tub is the best way to end the day.

Young Jae's hot tub is huge, more like a mini swimming pool than anything. Steam rises into the cold air as we pile in, settling around the perimeter on the seats.

The stars are vibrant above us, and the stillness of the mountain night is incredibly peaceful.

"There's drinks in the cooler." Young Jae motions to a huge cooler set into what looks like a custom holder next to the hot tub.

Sighing as a jet massages my lower back, I watch Rae chatting with Elise and Adeline, her smile brilliant as she tilts her head back and laughs.

With a sly smile, Rae turns to us. "We should keep the fun going with a game of truth or dare."

"If we're playing truth or dare, I definitely need a drink," Owen says, catching my eye and tossing me a beer when I nod.

Young Jae drinks deeply before saying, "Well, I'm not going first."

Adeline volunteers to go first, selecting dare, which surprises me, but when I look around, I realize no one else is. Looking at the quiet woman I barely know and seeing her in a different light, I watch as she laughs when Elise dares her to do a seductive dance for Owen, and she does it readily.

Owen stares at her the entire time, and I realize he's in love with her. I know enough from little things that Rae has said that they're not there yet, but he is.

We cycle through a few rounds with funny but easy tasks.

"Elise, you're up! Truth or dare." Rae grins as she does a little twirl in the water before flopping down next to me. Chuckling as her drink almost goes under, I catch her as she slips.

"Oops. I think I'm done with the drinks for tonight. I forgot how much being in a hot tub impacts how they hit you." She laughs, setting her drink on the edge.

We turn back to the game as Elise chooses truth.

Young Jae throws out casually, "What's your biggest goal this year?"

She mutters something I miss other than the word "single." Glancing around, I know I'm not the only one who heard it, but no one looks especially surprised.

Clearing her throat, she says, "My goal is to do one thing a month that I've wanted to do but have been too scared."

She turns to me, her cheeks a little flushed. "Truth or dare, Cam."

Looking around at my tipsy friends, I grin. "Dare."

Elise thinks for a moment, glancing between me and Rae. "I dare you to give in to the thing you want most right now."

Grinning, I turn to Rae and pull her onto my lap, kissing her deeply to loud hoots and hollers from our friends. She kisses me back until we're both breathless and then slides back down to where she was sitting next to me.

Moving on, I challenge Owen and the game continues until one by one someone heads in to bed until I'm outside alone with Owen.

"I like Adeline. She's good for you."

He has a look of complete bliss on his face. "She is. It didn't start out that way, but there was no denying the attraction."

"I heard she almost crashed into you." The story of Adeline's first run-in with Owen is still something the gossip mill likes to talk about. Although, at the same time, it's become apparent the town is fond of her.

He shakes his head, his lips twitching. "Yeah, she was trying to find the place, and her navigation was confused, so she was looking at it and, well, long story short, our introduction was me telling her she should go back where she came from."

Chuckling, I nod. "Yeah, I can see how that would go over."

"Then, one day, she calls me up with a plumbing emergency. I walk in, she's soaked head to toe, and her main floor bathroom is flooding." He grimaces and says, "On her phone, she has a YouTube video playing from some plumber Joe or something idiotic."

Snorting, I mutter, "You're joking, right?"

"She asked me for help to renovate the house, admitting she couldn't do it on her own. I didn't want to say yes, but looking at her soaking wet and dejected, I couldn't say no."

Laughing, I can picture the scene right down to the scowl on Owen's face. "Sounds like you stepped in at the right time!"

"It seemed like she was on the brink of disaster. In the beginning, I did everything I could to avoid being there. At the time, I told myself it was because she would be in the way and annoying, but deep down, I knew it was because she had thrown me for a loop. My heart belonged to her long before my head caught up." His smile changes to a softer one. One of pure love.

"Damn, I'm so happy for you." Yawning, I excuse myself. "Well, I think I better call it. See you in the morning."

Making a dash for the cabin, I towel myself off before heading to the shower. The entire time I'm in there I think about how happy Owen is. He hasn't always been lucky in love and for him to find someone as awesome as Adeline, he deserves it. I sure hope Rae and I can get there, and find that same kind of happiness.

I'm sitting on my bed in fresh sweats when a soft knock sounds on my door.

"Come in."

It swings open, Raelynn looking adorable in an oversized T-shirt.

"I just wanted to say goodnight." Her voice is low as she eyes me in my sweats.

Standing, I close the distance between us and pull her into my arms, shutting the door behind her. "You sleeping in here tonight?"

She nods against my chest, her eyes glimmering as she looks up at me.

CHAPTER
Sixteen

RAELYNN

My doorbell rings, interrupting a thrilling evening of catching up on laundry and the reality TV I've been devouring.

Mocha stops bathing herself long enough to judge me as I push up off the floor with a groan, hitting pause as two men realize they're interested in the same woman.

The bell rings again as I head down the hall. "Hold on, I'm coming," I call.

Opening the door, I blink in surprise when Elise and Adeline are on the other side.

We just got home from the cabin a few nights ago.

Before I can say anything, they're holding up beer and wings, sliding past me.

"We came bearing goodies. We need the deets on what happened between you and Cam. The CliffsNotes you gave us when we arrived was not enough." Elise practically sashays down the hall into my living room. "Ooo, I've been watching this. It's chaos, and I love it."

Adeline smirks when she sees the reality dating show paused on my screen. "Even Owen can't walk away when I watch this. He's hooked even though he says he doesn't like it."

We settle around my coffee table, shoving my laundry aside and laying out the food.

"Now dish. Because we know there's more that went down other than one hook up and a talk." Elise refocuses on me, her gaze intense.

Laughing, I shrug. "That's the gist of it. The first night, we got a little tipsy and ended up in bed. Which led to a bit of awkwardness the next day. It wasn't until the evening that we talked, or I guess fought about everything." Pausing, I look between them. "He and Sarah didn't start dating until several years after they met. They were friends first."

I go in-depth about what we talked about and the days that followed until they joined us.

"We slept together every night, and before we came home, we agreed to take it slow and try again. We don't really want the external forces in our relationship just yet. We agreed to either meet out of town or here for now. At least until we feel like we have our footing again." I can't stop the smile. We've been talking every day and saw each other last night. It feels like I'm in a dream.

Elise's voice is high when she squeals, "This is huge!"

She's practically bursting with excitement.

"How do you anticipate being able to keep the rumor

mill from spinning? What about your neighbors?" Adeline's voice is soft, practical. I can tell she's excited, but she knows how it feels to have her relationship under the microscope. Elise and Jake have been together long enough that they fly under the radar.

"It helps with winter. He will park in the garage so his car isn't in my driveway. And outside of town, it's a bit easier. Last night we found this place about an hour away that is decorated with dirty gnomes. It's hilarious." I laugh, recounting the few that stuck out the most.

They both look a little skeptical.

"That can't be real," Adeline mutters, pulling out her phone.

"It is. Look up Mistik Ridge. It's even part of their town website now." I pick at the wings while they're distracted, chuckling over the charming story of how the gnomes originated.

Ten minutes later, Elise looks up, her expression amused. "Okay, I definitely need to go there. I doubt Jake would find it as entertaining though, so maybe a friend trip."

Adeline agrees, before shifting the subject back to me and Cam. "Have you talked with Cam about how to approach 'going public'? I don't want you to feel overwhelmed, but you know it will be big news."

Sighing, I nod. "We know that this bubble will be short-lived. We talked a bit about it and will likely have a hard launch to get it over and done with. But I'd like to be in our own world for a bit at least. Go on some dates and just enjoy each other."

She sips at her beer, eyes pensive. "Okay. As long as you're both ready for it. You need to do what feels right."

"And you know we are here to support you. We're fully on your team," Elise adds.

My heart feels full as we dive into fun, low-key date ideas that Cam and I can go on before turning on the reality show. By the time they head out for the evening, I feel even more hopeful about what's to come for me and Cam.

CHAPTER
Seventeen

CAMERON

Penelope comes into my office, frowning as she flips through a chart. "Mrs. Stevenson canceled her appointment for tomorrow. Word's out that Suzanne retired earlier than expected, and per Mrs. Stevenson's words, 'I'm team Raelynn.' That's the third person this week. Maybe you need to talk to Rae about this. You know how small towns are."

Leaning back in my chair, I take the file and nod. "You're right. And I know Rae wouldn't want people to do this."

"Yeah, the rumor mill is churning, and the town is split on whether you came back for the right reasons or not. As much as you're a part of this town too, they adjusted to you being away for so long." She crosses her arms, frowning. "What a nuisance. I don't understand people who would walk away from a good vet and drive an hour to get to the next closest one."

With a sigh, I press my fingers against my temple. It has been quieter than expected since getting back from the cabin. I just never thought that my relationship with Rae could be the cause. We've been keeping things pretty quiet, so I guess the town still thinks we're not on speaking terms, but damn.

The bell rings at the front and Penelope heads out of my office, shutting my door.

Picking up my cell, I call Rae.

She answers, her voice sounding tired. "Hey, Cam. Good timing, I just finished with a client."

"Are you free for lunch? You sound like you need a good meal as much as I do."

"Yeah, that sounds good. Do you want me to pick something up and bring it by the clinic?" She already sounds perkier, my headache easing a bit at the shift.

"I was thinking Cliff's. If you're okay with that?"

The line is quiet before she responds. "Are you sure?"

"I'm sure." My voice is emphatic. "It's time."

"Okay. I'm fine with that, it will be nice to be able to act normal. I couldn't be a spy or something like that, always watching where I go and what I do." She chuckles. "Let's meet in an hour. I need to get back to town and send in an offer."

We hang up, and things feel a bit lighter. I head into one of the examination rooms to check on a jittery rabbit.

"Pen, if you're good to clean things up for tomorrow, you can head home afterward. Full pay." Her eyes are worried as she nods, but she doesn't say anything.

Ashton and Rita already went home, the day too quiet to need them. I need to resolve things. Otherwise, my attempt at owning my own vet clinic will be short-lived.

An hour later, I'm sitting in a side booth waiting for Rae.

The rest of the patrons see her before I do, the murmur of chatter falling. Looking up, I see her scanning the room, smiling when she sees me.

She comes over, sliding into the booth across from me.

"Thanks." Rae holds up the drink I ordered for her.

I can feel eyes on us, and as Rae glances around, she shakes her head. "Now I know how Adeline felt when she first moved here."

I follow her gaze, shaking my head when the room fills with the sound of everyone talking at once. "Yeah, apparently, the town has picked sides."

Her brows furrow at my tone. "Did something happen?"

With a sigh, I lean forward. "I really didn't want to say anything. I thought it would even itself out, but we've had several cancellations over the past few weeks. When they cancel, they say it's because they're on your team. I figured it would settle down, but I guess our discreetly meeting has managed to escape the town's notice. They took it for us avoiding each other and not talking. I wouldn't ask you to do anything, but we had three more this week."

Raelynn's nose scrunches. "Ugh. I'm sorry, Cam. I will do what I can to get them off your back. I'm guessing that's why you wanted to meet here."

Reaching across the table, I squeeze her hand. "It was,

but I was also craving a burger. Anyway, I think even seeing us here and talking normally will help."

She smiles, the strain around her eyes easing. We both look out to the rest of the dining area, smirking at each other when people quickly look away. "I think your plan is working."

Relaxing in the booth, I give her a firm look. "We haven't seen much of each other this week. I was starting to think you've been avoiding me."

She shakes her head. "That's not it. I have been wrapping up a bunch of sales and in between there exploring a few things. It might take a bit of getting used to, being part of a couple again. I'm not used to checking in with anyone anymore."

I open my mouth to respond when my phone rings, Sarah's name coming up on the screen.

Raelynn's face goes blank as I swipe to answer, causing me to pause. "I'm sorry, I have to take this. I've been waiting for a call to find out if we finally have a buyer for the house."

"Hey, Sarah." My eyes don't leave Raelynn's face, but she has busied herself on her phone. I hate knowing that this is hurting her, but until the house sells, there's nothing I can do.

"Hey, I thought I would let you know the house has a couple offers. I'm going to send them your way via email, but one couple seems to be in a hurry. Their offer isn't the highest, but the turnaround would be fast. I've highlighted it in the email." She's typing as she speaks, her voice neutral.

"Is the offer worth it, even with the quickness of the

sale?" I appreciate that she wants it dealt with, but not to our detriment.

"Yeah, it's a good offer, and the couple with the highest offer has a lot more contingencies." Her voice is confident, helping ease my concern.

"Okay, send them my way. I trust your judgment on this. Thanks for dealing with everything. I appreciate it. I will look at the email when I'm back at the clinic."

We hang up, Rae setting her phone down and meeting my gaze. Her brown eyes are cautious. "Why did you and Sarah end the relationship?"

Her question shouldn't be a surprise, but I'm taken aback.

"We sat down to dinner one night, and she mentioned talking about starting a family, and my immediate reaction was to shut it down. I realized then that if I couldn't have a family with you, I didn't want it with anyone else. As I told her I didn't want to, we started delving deeper into it. She said she wasn't upset by that, and she felt like she should be because she's always wanted kids. The discussion progressed from there to us agreeing we were better as friends, and we filed for a simple divorce the next day." Gesturing to my phone, I say, "We thought we had sold the house, but it ended up falling through, so Sarah has been communicating with the Realtor. I guess we have a few new offers on the house, and she wanted to let me know about one in particular."

She nods, leaning back as her body relaxes. "That makes sense. And I'm glad you were able to end things so well."

It hurts to see her so on guard after the progress we

made at the cabin, but I get it. "I can't take away what was done, Rae. And I understand your hurt and will work through it however I can. Sarah didn't do anything wrong and until things are settled completely, I can't just cut her out."

Her eyes flash, her lips pressing together as she stares at me before spitting out, "Did I ask you to? I never said anything that would give the idea that I can't handle any remaining things that need to be settled between you and Sarah. However, I am allowed to sit with whatever feelings I have when something comes up, and if it's anything that needs discussing, I will let you know. That felt accusatory, and it's not fair."

She crosses her arms, silence filling between us as the server comes and takes our orders. I can feel eyes on us, but all I care about is Rae.

"You're right. That was unfair." Running my hand over my head, I groan. "Thank you for calling me out on it."

She chuckles, the remaining tension leaving her face. "You're welcome."

Our food comes and we find our way back to easy conversation as we eat. I can feel the eyes of the other patrons on us throughout our meal and know that soon the gossip train will make its rounds.

"What are your thoughts on making plans with Owen and Adeline? She seems really nice. Owen told me about how they met. I have to admit I am curious to see the house." Shoving my plate aside, I watch Raelynn's eyes close in bliss as she finishes her burger.

She catches my gaze and grins. "You know damn well how good these are."

"I do. I just love watching you enjoy your food."

She rolls her eyes. "And yes, let's make plans with Adeline and Owen. She's become one of my best friends, and if we can learn from anyone how to move on from hurt, it's her. I will call her later and set it up."

Her work phone rings, and she sighs when she sees the name on the ID. "I need to go. This client is particularly difficult, so the sooner I get him off my list the better."

"I've got lunch. You head out and I will talk to you later."

She smiles gratefully as she answers the call, her customer service voice taking over as she rushes out the door.

After paying I head back to the clinic, wondering if maybe I need to ask Suzanne to stay on longer. As I walk in the door, Penelope comes out of the back.

"I don't know what you did, but Mrs. Stevenson called and rebooked her appointment, as have half the other clients who canceled. I was about to leave when the phone started ringing." The phone rings, and she rushes to answer it. Looking up from the caller ID, she mouths, "And another one."

Grinning, I head to my office to call Ashton and Rita.

CHAPTER
Eighteen

RAELYNN

Cam stops his car outside Adeline's gate, moving to get out.

Hand on his arm, I say, "I will get the gate. Kane and Stella need introductions before they let you on the property."

He looks at the gate and sees the two Turkish Kangal guard dogs staring out at him, and he nods.

We park outside the house and I introduce him to the dogs. They're massive and loving but won't let anyone near Adeline without proper introductions first.

"I'm guessing there's a story behind those two." He scratches them on the head before following me up to the porch. He finally processes the house and looks at me, eyes wide. "This is not the house I remember."

Chuckling, I nod. "Yeah, her vision and Owen's hard

work, along with many contractors, and it's a beautiful home again."

As I enter the house, I fill him in on the story that led to Owen picking up the pups and dropping them off.

Owen comes to greet us, catching the end of my story. "Yep, no other woman would think to chase a cougar off her property, but all Adeline could think of was it making a smorgasbord of the non-existent kittens in her barn."

Adeline yells from the kitchen, "There may not have been any at that time, but you know we've found more than one kitten in there."

Laughing, I follow Owen to where Adeline lays out a delicious looking spread. There are lobster tails, steaks, salmon, and asparagus, and she keeps adding more food.

"How many of us are coming?" I laugh as I give her a hug while Owen shows Cam some of the upgrades around the house.

Adeline hands me a glass of wine as the guys stop in front of the photo collage wall in her living room. I see Cam pause at her wedding photo.

She walks over there, handing him a glass. "That's my late husband, Scott. He passed away fifteen months ago."

Owen wraps his arm around Adeline, kissing her temple.

Cam looks between them. His expression is carefully neutral. "That's a hard loss. I'm sorry."

Adeline's smile is soft, her eyes sad as she leans her head into Owen's chest. "It was. A drunk driver hit him."

Cam swears under his breath, shaking his head. Looking back at the photo. "People will never learn, will they?"

Adeline agrees, looking back at the photo. "His loss was hard, but I know he's with me. And he would be so happy for me and the life I've created here."

Adeline kisses Owen on the cheek, moving back into the kitchen.

"Wow, I can't even imagine," Cam murmurs, looking at Owen.

I can see he's checking to see how Owen feels about that.

"She is who she is because of her life leading up to now, and I love her more for it." Owen grins, his eyes drawn to the woman loading more food onto the table. "Now, let's attempt to make a dent in the meal she made before it gets cold."

We sit down, diving in.

"This is amazing! Thank you for hosting us," Cam says as he sits down.

Owen serves Adeline, his gaze approving when Cam does the same for me. "How are things at the clinic?"

Cam pauses, glancing at me. "It was a bit touch and go after Suzanne decided to retire earlier than expected. Clients were canceling because they were, and I quote, 'Team Raelynn,' but Rae and I went to lunch at Cliff's and since then it's picking back up."

Grimacing, I add, "Yeah, I had to tell a few people to stop being ridiculous. I understand they want to show their support, but that's not the way to do it. Even if we weren't—where we're at, even I took my cat to see Cam."

"It still boggles my mind how everyone knows every-one. It weirds me out when someone greets me by name and I've never met them." Adeline shudders a bit. "Especially considering my introduction to town."

She fills Cam in on how she first met Owen.

Cam laughs. "Oh, I know. I heard."

Adeline blushes, dropping her head into her hands. "Oh god."

We all chuckle as we tell Adeline different stories of when we were the center of the town gossip. Growing up in Willowbrook Lake, it's happened multiple times. By the end, we're all laughing.

Standing, I scowl at Adeline when she starts to clear the table. "I've got this."

Owen gets up to help me as Cam and Adeline move to the living room and chat.

"You look happy," Owen murmurs as we wash dishes.

Smiling, I shrug. "I am. We're taking it slow and there are things that need to be done, but I think we will get there."

He nudges me. "You will. I know you will."

We join Adeline and Cam in the living room when the kitchen is clean.

"I don't have any board games. When I packed my old house, I wasn't in the best space and I got rid of a lot of things that hurt to look at and remember." She looks embarrassed, but before Owen or I can say anything, Cam jumps in.

"That's understandable. Sometimes, to protect ourselves, our minds do things out of the ordinary to cope. I'm enjoying just sharing in conversation with the woman who has Owen so enraptured." Cam leans back, laying his arm over the back of the couch, his fingers playing with my hair.

Adeline beams at us as Nora, Adeline's three-legged cat, hops into her lap, curling up and going to sleep.

The entire time we visit, it feels like no time has passed and nothing has changed. It's an amazing feeling, but I know that things aren't the same and I need to put in the work that Adeline has so I can be the best version of me. For Cam. For myself.

CHAPTER
Nineteen

RAELYNN

Mocha purrs on my lap as I peruse the website. It's easy, the messaging is direct, and the reviews are good.

Licking my lips, I open the intake form. The grief counselor has phenomenal reviews in the infertility group I'm in, but I've never bothered to take the step to connect with her. I've done other counseling to help manage my regret from ending things and the hurt I had at Cam for moving on so fast but looking back, I realize that I wasn't really doing the work. Seeing Cam again, seeing where it goes, means I need to do the work. I can't handle what occurred last time happening again.

My work phone rings, a client's name popping up on the screen. We're in the process of closing on a house, and he has become insufferable the closer we get.

"Hello, Raelynn speaking."

"Yeah, it's Brian. I'm still waiting for the documents to sign. What's going on?" His tone is rude, instantly raising my hackles. He had the red flags of a difficult client, but I ignored them and have regretted it every day since.

Taking a deep breath, I close my eyes and with my most professional voice say, "I know Brian, but as we discussed this morning, we're waiting on the lawyer. And they can take three to four business days to draft every-thing and send it off. It's not instant."

He's silent for a moment, but I know better than to get my hopes up. The man doesn't listen. "Yeah, that's not going to work for me."

Firmly, I respond, "Well, you could find a new lawyer, which could take days, and then ask them to do it, but their turnaround will be the same. If you like, I can send him an email now telling him we no longer need his services."

Tapping on my computer, I smirk when he panics. "No! No, it's okay. A few days isn't a big deal."

"Wonderful. I will let you know once I receive the documents. Have a good rest of your day." Hanging up, I turn my work phone off and bang my forehead on my desk.

Shaking my body, I coo at Mocha when she meeps at me. "Sorry, baby. That is why I'm looking at courses. Today. I'm done with this."

Filling out the intake form for the grief counselor, I close it out before opening the course catalog from a local university that offers online classes.

My head starts spinning as I scroll through different options and realize how many there are.

Picking up my cell, I call Adeline.

"Hey. Good timing. I wanted to tell you how much I enjoyed our double date. I like Cam. I can see why he's held such a special place in your heart all these years."

Smiling, I sink back into my chair. Since I first met her, something about Adeline has made me feel so at ease. It didn't take long for her to become one of the most important people in my life. "Yes, I'm just glad we have a chance to work it out. I never thought it would happen. But I actually called for a different reason."

Concern immediately fills her voice. "Is everything okay?"

"Yeah, I think I'm finally ready to move into a different career, I'm just not happy anymore, and life is too short to work a job that drains you." She hums in agreement. "But I started looking at courses, and there are just so many. It's overwhelming and I don't really know how to start."

"Why did you get into real estate in the first place?"

Memories of my dad going through cancer treatments flood me. My mom was having a hard time maintaining it, so I adjusted my plans. "Honestly, the fact that there was a training course offered close by so I could help my mom while my dad went through cancer treatment. I really wanted to go to college for graphic design, but there weren't the same options for learning online that there are now."

Cam went to college about an hour away and stayed living in Willowbrook Lake so we didn't have to do long distance. He helped us out so much during that time.

"Wow. That's a big decision to make." Adeline's soft voice pulls me from my memories.

"I like being a Realtor, I do. But I'm just now realizing that I resent it too because it's not what I want." I feel guilty even saying this, it was my decision, and no one is responsible for that but myself, and yet looking back I was young and felt like I really didn't have a choice.

She hums softly. "It sounds like you already know what you want to do. If graphic design is still something that interests you, I say go for it. Especially since it's a lot easier to find courses online."

Taking a deep breath, I put her on speaker and search for options. As we chat, I submit my application to a school offering comprehensive courses online before searching for free online tutorials to get me started.

"Thank you. I really appreciate you." I relax a bit, closing my laptop to give Adeline my full attention. "We should plan a girls' night with Elise. It's been a while."

"I agree, and I feel like she needs some time to relax. I saw her this morning when I popped in for a coffee, and she seemed stressed." Adeline's voice is concerned.

I've noticed the same. Things with Jake seem to be getting worse, not better, but she still won't call it quits. "I think she's scared to start over. She lives in his house, and if she left, it would mean starting almost from scratch."

She hums sympathetically. "I get it."

We talk a while longer before saying goodbye. Hanging up, I lift Mocha and kiss her head. "I'm not going to spend my life living with regrets. I can't change the past, but I sure as hell can change my future."

And maybe one day Elise will see she can too.

CHAPTER
Twenty

RAELYNN

Cam's arms flail as his skates slide from under him, and he crashes onto the ice. Covering my mouth, I stifle a giggle. "Should I get you one of those skating buddies? All the little kids seem to be doing great pushing those around."

He scowls before we both burst into laughter. "I might need a walker after this. I thought it would be like riding a bike."

"It should be. Maybe in your old age, you've lost your coordination." Gliding past him, I rotate so I'm skating backward past him.

His brows furrow, but his eyes shine. "We're the same age."

"Um, excuse me, you're four months older than I am." Planting my hands on my hips, I sass, "And apparently, thirty-three years old for me is not the same as thirty-three years old for you, old man."

His arm shoots out, catching me behind the knees as I go to pass him again. He catches me as I fall, somehow managing to get me onto his lap.

Cam smirks. "Lacking coordination, my ass. I'm pretty sure these skates need to be sharpened, seeing as they were in the same box I packed them into when I moved."

Pain flickers in his eyes, but it's gone before I can say anything, so I move past it. "Well, now that you're back, we better rectify that."

The air between us thickens, his hand cupping the back of my head as he pulls my lips to his. Despite the soft brush of his lips, my entire body burns with need.

When we agreed to take things slow, we hadn't discussed it, but we haven't been intimate since the cabin over a month ago. Our time together has been wonderful, and fun, and I have loved getting to know Cam again, but it's hard to remove the physical from our relationship.

Sighing as he pulls away, I smack his shoulder gently as he smirks.

"I meant to tell you, I signed up for a graphic design course. It starts in March." Licking my lips, I brush some ice off my pants. "And I am starting grief counseling for infertility next week. I had a counselor before, but I realized it wasn't the best fit for my needs. Hopefully, this one will be better."

Cam pulls me into his arms, holding me tight. "I hope so too. If there's anything you need from me, don't hesitate to say something."

Nodding into his neck, I breathe him in. "I will."

———

Cam gets an emergency call at the clinic, effectively ending our date early. In my boredom, I decide to head to my parents' house.

Momma opens the door, smiling brightly when she sees me. "Baby!"

She pulls me into her arms and her hug envelopes me. "Hi, Momma. How are you and Dad doing?"

She guides me into the house, sighing. "I wish that man would retire already. I'm ready to downsize."

Chuckling as I follow her into the kitchen, she immediately starts pulling things out to cook. "He barely slowed down when he was getting chemo. Why would you think he would now?"

She turns to me, arching a brow. "Oh, he will. That man only listens to one person and that's me."

"That's the truth." My dad's voice fills the room as he comes down the hall. "Hi, sweetheart. What brings you by?"

He pulls me in and kisses me on the forehead.

My parents are polar opposites. Mom tends to be the more easygoing of the two until she's upset or in momma bear mode. She loves to joke and laugh, wants adventure, and is a staple around town on various committees.

My dad, on the other hand, tends to be more stoic, but when Momma is upset, he's the only one who can bring her down. His jokes are dryer than hers, but he always makes her laugh. Despite loving the small-town living, he hates small town involvement and tends to stay on the farm.

Somehow, despite their differences, the two of them have the most solid relationship I know.

"I'm sure you've heard that Cam is back in town. And the town gossip channels have probably also told you we've been seen together. I wanted to let you know we're trying again." Holding my breath, I wait for them to come back with some concern or another.

They didn't know the extent of my heartbreak, but enough that they haven't brought him up since he left.

They look at each other before both of their eyes are on me. Finally, Dad says, "We always liked Cam, and we know you. If you're giving it a shot, then we know it's right."

Breathing a sigh of relief, I relax a little. My parents try not to give their opinion without being asked, but it's still important for me to have their support.

Momma nods. "Honestly, we thought he would come back sooner, but maybe you both needed other life experiences to realize what you had was real, and you can make it through anything."

Smiling, I stand and give them both hugs. "Thank you for always supporting me."

Washing my hands, I join Momma in the kitchen and help her make dinner as Dad heads out to do evening chores.

A couple hours later we hear the garage door open just as we finish setting everything on the table.

"Look who showed up," Dad says as he walks in, James on his heels.

We meet each other's eyes and start laughing. It's been

since Christmas that we all sat down as a family, which is unusual. "We didn't even discuss this."

James ruffles my hair. "We don't need to, sis. The town does it for us. Everyone is talking about you and Cam making out on the ice and then heading this way. The speculation is flowing."

Groaning, I roll my eyes. "We were not making out."

My brother laughs, sitting down at the table. Momma smacks his hands.

"Go and wash up!"

He gets up, fully chastised as we sit and wait for him. When he comes back, he sits down and throws a roll at me when he sees the smug grin on my face.

Dad clears his throat, and we all start to dish up, James filling us in on his day.

"We've been seeing an increase in vandalism around town, so the chief wants me to go to the high school for their next assembly. He thinks I will connect better with the kids than some of the other officers." He shrugs it off, but I know how hard he's worked to get the reputation he has.

Teasing him about being the "hot cop" as I've heard so many people call him, I think back to when he first joined the force. Willowbrook Lake has always been a fairly accepting town, especially since our town council has a zero tolerance for racism. Despite that, James is still the only Black cop in town. Our force is small, five cops, the chief, and their admin. He was always accepted amongst his peers, but I know a few older residents pushed back against it. It was a hard time, our perspective of the town took a hit, but it was a very small minority of people.

Glancing at my dad, I remember one time I saw him truly get mad. He went to a town meeting where those people decided to protest and gave them a lecture. The majority of the town backed him up, but the mayor still changed the agenda for the remainder of the meeting to address racism and discrimination. That's also when the town council decided to create the committee on inclusion that Momma heads.

It made me so proud to be a part of such an inclusive community.

Those few people eventually faded away and it hasn't been an issue since. James has an incredible reputation around town, and I would guess he may become chief one day.

"I think that's a good idea. The town is growing." Momma smiles, pride filling her gaze.

We finish our meal, my family supporting my decision to take courses and change my career. I know my parents feel guilty about my college plans changing, but I don't regret it. Thankfully, I'm in a position to be able to change things, even if it's nerve-racking.

As I head home that evening, I think about all the changes coming my way. It's a lot, but despite some fear of failure, I'm mostly excited about the possibilities.

CHAPTER
Twenty~One

RAELYNN

Parking my car outside the clinic, I glance at the time. Ten minutes. My stomach is in knots, and I can feel my pulse thrumming everywhere.

Breathing deeply, I check my phone only to see it's about to die. *Damn.*

Getting out of the car, I stretch. The infertility counselor I found travels to you if she can find a space available and you're within an hour's drive for the first session. After that, the sessions usually move to virtual. It was important to me to meet her in person first, but the idea of driving home after something I can only guess will be intensely emotional was not ideal. Thankfully, she could rent a room for the hour at the doctor's clinic in town.

The bell dings as I open the door, April smiling when she sees me. "Raelynn, is everything okay?"

"Yes, everything is fine. I have an appointment with Dr. Fletcher."

Awareness fills her gaze, and she asks me to take a seat.

I'm not waiting long before a motherly looking woman with honey blond hair French braided down her back emerges. She has a round, soft face, and when she smiles, I instantly feel comfortable.

"Raelynn, it's nice to meet you. Come inside and get comfortable." I follow her into a cozy room filled with plants and a couple of armchairs.

Sitting in one next to a huge monstera, I lace my fingers together and wait as she goes to a sidebar.

"Would you like some tea or coffee?" she asks, pouring herself a coffee.

Surprise takes away some of the nerves. Clearing my throat, I say, "Tea, please, peppermint if you have it."

Dr. Fletcher hands me a cup with a little plate that has honey, sugar, cream, and a stir stick. Nothing about this is like my previous experience, and I'm more at ease than I expected.

"Now, let's talk about what led you to reach out and your goals. I want you to get the most out of our sessions possible." She sits in the chair adjacent to mine, sipping her coffee.

Setting my mug down, I try to think of how to phrase all the chaos in my head. "Five years ago, my then boyfriend and I were trying to have a baby. We had been for a couple years and received news that it would be extremely difficult, but we decided to keep trying."

Running my hands over my jeans, I look at her and she gestures to keep going.

"It was endless disappointments and it felt like Cam was shutting down, so I quit trying to talk about my own pain to shelter him. Ultimately, I ended the relationship because it was all too much." Picking up my mug, I take a sip.

Dr. Fletcher nods, her expression soft. "Infertility can often take a big toll on relationships. It's something I hear often."

Sighing, I tuck one knee into myself. It helps knowing we're not alone in our struggles.

"Now he's back in town, and we're rebuilding our relationship. I just want to deal with it because I don't want it to destroy our chance. Part of me worries he will regret not having children, even though he says he's fine with it. And I can't go through that entire process again." My breath whooshes out of me. It's hard to express exactly how I feel when it's been so long, but I know I need the help.

She nods, thoughtful. "Sometimes it's hard to reconcile the hopes of our past selves with where we're at now. Has he given any indication that when he says he's okay not having a child it's untrue?"

Her question makes me pause. His relationship with Sarah ended because of her question about family planning, and Cam has never lied to me about anything. Shaking my head no, I whisper, "I want—wanted—to give him a family so bad."

"When you picture your family, what do you see right now?"

Thinking, I picture my life and my family. "My parents and brother, Cam, and my circle of friends. Oh, and my cat Mocha."

"When you think of that picture, does it feel incomplete?" Dr. Fletcher asks, her tone gentle but neutral.

Taking a deep breath, I close my eyes and really think about how I feel. My life is full, I'm enjoying my classes. I've been doing more photography. And when I imagine the plans Cam and I have, I realize that I'm content. As things are. "No. They don't. I'm content. I mean, I wouldn't mind getting another cat one day, but the rest feels okay."

She smiles and I feel her warmth wash over me. "Well, that's a great start. Sometimes we hang on to pictures of how we think our life should be instead of focusing on how it is and what it can be."

Floored, I nod slowly. Somehow, this reframe has helped shift my perspective. I don't think I'm magically cured of my little triggers, but she is spot on. I've held on to this picture of what the perfect life with Cam would be like, but if I reflect back to before we started trying to have a baby, our life was good and full. And I tossed it out like it was nothing.

"Wow. I never thought about it like that before. It's hard not to look at the decision I made to end our relationship with even more regret though, knowing that. I took something truly wonderful and threw it away." My voice chokes and I feel tears well in my eyes.

She hums softly. "I think we've come to the real root of your grief. Of course part of it is the sadness for the baby you wanted and don't have, but beyond that, when you speak about your life, you have more emotion over the loss of your relationship rather than the lack of a child in your life."

Adjusting myself in the chair, I think about the disappointment over the pregnancy tests. It was real and intense, but when I think of my regret over the past five years, it's always centered around Cam.

We delve deeper into the last two years of my relationship with Cam and the hour is up before I know it.

"Raelynn, I am happy to continue to meet here if you prefer to meet in person, or we can do it virtually, whichever you prefer. Just email me to confirm a few days before our next appointment." Dr. Fletcher stands as I do and we walk out.

"Sounds good. Thank you."

Heading out the door, my body feels tired. The session was amazing but draining at the same time.

As I approach my car, I hear my name. "Raelynn! Wait up."

Looking up, I see Carol approaching. She's an assistant at the school and is heavily involved in organizing events around town.

"Hey, Carol. How are you?"

She's huffing for breath when she stops next to my car. "I'm okay, but how are you?" The way she emphasizes you is weird.

"I'm fine…"

"Okay. I was just curious. I was in Perk Up and wondered if you knew who the pretty woman Cam was hugging is. They looked pretty friendly." She chatters on, but my heart is sinking. "I think I heard him call her Sarah. Isn't that his ex-wife? They looked pretty comfortable together."

I don't think Cam would cheat on me, but it hurts that

he wouldn't give me a heads-up that they're meeting. In a town that loves to gossip.

"That could be. I, uh, I have a meeting I need to get to. It was good to see you." Excusing myself, I hop into my car and head home.

CHAPTER
Twenty-Two

CAMERON

"She can go into kennel four. Make sure you call the family and let them know her spay went well and they should be able to pick her up in a few hours." My team nods as they start to clean up the operating room. "She seems to be doing okay with the anesthetic, but keep an eye on her for any changes."

I wash up and head into my office, glancing at my cell hoping for a message from Rae.

Instead, one is waiting for me from Sarah letting me know she will be coming to town at noon to get the papers for the house signed. She asked me to meet her at Perk Up.

Glancing at the time, I groan. "Shit."

Taking off my white coat, I grab my jacket and tell Penelope I have to run a quick errand as I head out the door. The door shuts behind me and I start dialing Sarah.

"Hey! I just saw your message. I didn't realize you were coming out today."

"Yeah, my day cleared so I figured I would bring it so we can get it done. I'm already at Perk Up and working, so whenever you can get here is fine. The coffee is incredible." Her voice is friendly, but I know that it hurts her that I've pulled away since coming back to town and reconnecting with Rae. We chat once in a while, but it's mostly when she initiates, which has been less and less as time goes on. It hurts me to hurt the person who has gotten me through so much, but I don't think I can navigate staying friends with my ex-wife while trying to rebuild my relationship with Raelynn.

"I will be there in five."

Perk Up is busy, the parking out front is full, so I pull around to the back as I try to call Rae. I go straight to voicemail. Crap. Leaving a quick message, I also send her a text.

The bell jingles as I enter, reminding me of my first day back in town, except this time Elise smiles at me, and aside from a couple quick glances, no one stares. Except Sarah.

"The usual?" Elise asks, quickly whipping up a flat white when I nod.

"Have you heard from Rae this afternoon?" I ask as she hands me my cup.

Elise nods. "She had some last-minute showings and then her counseling appointment."

Right, I forgot today was her first one.

Glancing at Sarah, I look back at Elise. "Before you go into protective mode. Sarah is here to get some final papers signed. We parted as friends, so if we're smiling and being friendly, don't think it's something it's not. It's last minute, and I haven't had a chance to tell Rae. I will, but I know you have girl code or whatever it is, so if you can hold off until I have a chance, I would appreciate it."

Her lips press into a firm line, but she nods.

Taking a deep breath, I walk to where Sarah is sitting and join her.

"You look good. Happy." She smiles and despite everything, it reaches her eyes. "I'm glad."

Smiling, I say, "You too. How have you been?"

She hands me the folder, glancing around as she notices everyone looking at us before they all look away. Rolling my eyes, I chuckle as she whispers, "They're not subtle, are they?"

Jerking my head in a shake, I sign the forms for the house. Handing them over, I ask again, "So, how have you been?"

"I'm glad these buyers are wanting a quick possession. It couldn't have come at a better time." She tucks the folder into her oversized bag. "My company asked me to relocate to their East Coast office. It comes with a big raise and relocation bonus."

"That's great! Congratulations." My enthusiasm is real.

Resting her chin in her hand, she looks at me. "I'm glad I met you, Cam. I know being here is where you need to be. But I hope you know I'm always here for you as a friend. And I don't regret anything."

Sarah stands before I can reply, so I stand too, and pull her into a hug. "Ditto."

She heads out the door.

It's true, I don't regret our friendship. All my regret lies in allowing Rae to walk away.

Glancing at the time, I rush back to the clinic to finish my day, hoping I can connect with Rae before the town gossip gets to her.

———

Penelope is the last to leave, locking up as I finish a few things in my office. Glancing at my phone, I see Rae still hasn't called me back. Cleaning up my desk, I call her, but after a few rings, I go to voicemail.

Sighing, I head into my apartment, strip down, and take a quick shower before throwing on some sweats and a hoodie.

Less than thirty minutes since my last call, I'm at Rae's front door, ringing the bell.

She lets me in, her expression closed off as she heads back down the hall without a word. Kicking off my shoes, I follow her, sitting right next to her on the couch.

"Be mad about it, but don't shut me out. We made a promise." I reach out to take her hand.

She finally meets my gaze. "I'm not mad. I just wish I hadn't heard about it through the town's grapevine. A heads-up would've been nice, so I could've mentally prepared myself for the speculation."

"I left a voicemail and sent a text."

She smacks her hand on her forehead. "My cell died while I was in my appointment. When I got home, I plugged in my phone but haven't checked it since."

"I didn't know until today that she was coming, otherwise I would have told you sooner." I cup her chin, stroking my thumb over her lips. "You're really not mad?"

She turns her head and kisses my palm. "No. I knew at some point you would see her to sign the paperwork. It was just a lot to leave my counseling appointment, and the first person I saw asked if I knew the pretty woman you were hugging at Perk Up."

Groaning, I shake my head and roll my eyes. The people in this town mean well, but shit, they lack awareness some days. "Yeah, that's shitty timing."

"I hate to admit I was jealous. It's still hard for me, sometimes, that you were married." Her voice lowers, her eyes dropping to her hands.

I sigh. "I know. And I know there's nothing I can do or say to make it better. But we both have things from the past five years. It seemed to me we had moved past a lot of this."

She looks up at me, her gaze clear. "We have. I'm not holding it against you. It was a knee-jerk reaction that I think will take some time to dissipate. Today was just a bad day for it all to come up, right after baring my soul about infertility and our relationship."

"That makes sense. I'm sorry I couldn't be there for you after. And that this meeting has somehow eclipsed that." I open my arms to her.

"How did the meeting go?" Rae asks, curling into me.

"Well, the house is sold, and they take possession in three weeks, so all our business is done. And people can put their noses back where they belong."

Raelynn pulls out of my arms and straddles me, cupping my cheeks. "Are you okay?"

Lifting my hips, I grin. "Right now, I'm better than okay."

She laughs, smacking my shoulder. "That's not what I meant, and you know it. Be serious."

My head drops to the back of the couch. "I'm okay. I knew this was coming and you're the most important person to me. Is it unfortunate that I'm losing out on my friendship with Sarah? Yes. But that's because of our decision to start a relationship rather than stay friends. We said goodbye, and everything is good."

She nods, chewing on her lower lip.

"How about you? It was a big day for you too." Running my hands up and down her arms, I watch her carefully.

She breathes out heavily. "It was hard. Intense, but in a good way. I don't know if that makes sense."

"Kind of. Do you want to talk about it?"

She thinks for a moment before giving a slow nod. "I talked a lot about the way it felt to have something we wanted so badly to be this perpetual disappointment. And I talked about my process in thinking about how it needed to be addressed and how we both coped." She pauses, her brown eyes on mine. "She helped me understand about coping, including giving me a few things to try if I ever feel triggered. I got more out of one session with her than I did in the entirety of time talking to my previous therapist."

"I'm glad. If there's ever a time you want me to go with you, I am there."

She nods, lost in thought for a moment before she grins and presses her hips into me.

"So, I know we've been going slow, but I think tonight we've proven that we've made progress in how we communicate. Want to stay?" She rotates her hips, moaning when she feels my erection.

Pulling her down, I kiss her hard. She wraps her arms around me, deepening the kiss as she grinds her hips into mine.

Pulling back, I stand with her in my arms and stride into her room, laying her on the bed.

"Fuck yes."

CHAPTER
Twenty-Three

RAELYNN
April

Class ends and I shut my laptop. I'm in the third week of classes and it's the best decision I've made. I found a course at a school that specializes in various arts, including graphic design. The best part about it is that the courses don't follow a regular college timeline and start at several points during the year, allowing me to start quickly. I got my acceptance, cut my hours, and have been happier than I can remember.

Glancing at my phone, I give Mocha a treat before grabbing my keys and heading out the door. Cam will be at the clinic late tonight, so I message Elise to let her know I'm on my way with wine.

She lives on the opposite side of town in an older home that her boyfriend, Jake, owned before they met. She moved in with him after a few months, but despite living there for four years, the house has never felt quite like hers. His car is in the driveway next to hers, so I pull around and park on the street.

The door is open, so I let myself in.

Jake's boots are in the middle of the floor instead of on the empty shoe rack. Putting my shoes away, I pick up his boots.

Elise has talked to him endless times about these little things, but he doesn't ever do anything differently. Jake's not a bad guy, but his lack of caring for the things that bother Elise rubs me the wrong way. She deserves better.

"I'm in the kitchen," Elise calls.

I join her, handing her the wine. "How was your day?"

She shrugs, glancing at where Jake lounges on the couch, completely engrossed in his phone. "Could be worse, could be better."

Grabbing a couple wine glasses, I gesture to the table. "I think you deserve that drink. Adeline said she will bring pizza later."

I fill her in on my courses and how counseling is going until Jake gets up.

"Babe, I'm going to go play pool with the guys. Be home late." He nods at me before heading out the door.

Elise's eyes are on the glass he left on the coffee table. She huffs out a breath and gets up to grab the glass. "He spent over an hour outside shoveling, which means he shoveled for twenty and then talked to the neighbor for the other forty. I cleaned the entire inside of the house. He came in and sat on the couch on his phone while I finished cleaning."

She presses her fingertips into her forehead.

"That's frustrating." I wish she would realize her worth and end things. I thought for a while that she might, but she always gives him more chances.

"I'm tired of having to repeat myself all the time. And then he says I just need to tell him, but I've tried that. It helps for a while, and then things go back to the way they were before." She drains her wine glass before pouring another. "And then I see you and Cam together. And Adeline and Owen. I realize that maybe it shouldn't be so hard."

Sipping at my wine, I nod. "I get it, it sucks when it's hard. Cam and I have been through hard times before, and we're in the honeymoon phase right now, but I don't think it will always remain this perfect. And you know that Adeline and Owen have worked hard to get to where they are. However, when you give someone feedback on how they make you feel, it should be respected. And you know Owen and Cam are pretty damn good at doing that."

She sighs. "You're right, relationships are work. I guess I mean in how Cam and Owen treat you both. I just wish that Jake would hear what I say and actually follow through on what I'm asking instead of making a joke about it or trying for a week and then going right back to the way it was. Maybe I just need to change my approach."

I'm about to backtrack, the last thing she needs to do is give that man more chances, but I'm interrupted as Adeline knocks, opening the door. "Pizza delivery!"

Elise straightens in her chair, smiling as Adeline enters with pizza and another bottle of wine.

Adeline looks between us, her excitement shifting to concern. "Is everything okay?"

Nodding, Elise shrugs off her mood. "Yeah, we were just talking about Jake, but I don't want to spend our evening dwelling. What are the guys up to today?"

"Owen and Young Jae just left to pick up Cam to go fishing." Adeline scrunches her nose. "I remember fishing with my dad. I don't know how they think it's fun."

We laugh.

"My dad used to try to take me too. It wasn't my thing." Elise chuckles. "I would just play with my toys on the pier."

Grimacing, I agree. "I don't enjoy it either, but I only went once with Cam and the guys. After an hour of boredom, I convinced them to swim instead."

"How is living with Owen going?" Elise asks Adeline as she grabs another slice of pizza.

Adeline flushes, pure joy written across her face. "Amazing. I didn't think it was possible to be this happy."

"And what about things at the shelter? Are you still enjoying it?"

Adeline's new job at the shelter wasn't a surprise to anyone. After the first several batches of abandoned kittens, she really wanted to do more than just drop them off.

"I love it. Oh, I mentioned that you're taking graphic design classes, so we may have some contract work for you if you're interested. The masquerade ball brought in an influx of donations, but it's hard being a charity in a small town." She leans back in her chair, talking about some of the upgrades the shelter needs.

We polish off the pizza and two bottles of wine.

Feeling buzzed, I suggest we play Twister and the girls agree.

"How are things going with Cam?" Adeline slides her foot onto the red.

I spin the wheel. "Elise, left hand yellow." Elise moves her hand with an unladylike grunt. "It's pretty good. We've been taking things slow, but I don't really want to. I want to go back to where we were before. It feels right, and I can't imagine not being with him again. I know what that's like, and it's not for me."

"I need to start yoga or something. This shouldn't be so hard." Elise shifts her weight a bit, trying to get comfortable. "It makes sense that it would be hard to go slow. You already have over ten years together, so starting from scratch is not the same."

We play until I fall, taking Adeline and Elise with me. By the time Jake gets home we've polished off another bottle and Adeline and I have both called for rides.

Owen picks Adeline up first.

"Owen, why don't we bring Twister home. We can play naked." Adeline giggles, lurching into his arms and wrapping herself around him.

Elise and I giggle. I hear Jake groan, but when I look over, I see he's still engrossed in his phone.

Scoffing, I roll my eyes.

Cam's voice comes through the front door. "Rae?"

"Come in!" I sing. "Before Adeline and Owen start stripping."

He comes down the hall, looking perplexed.

Owen groans, scooping Adeline into his arms. "I think it's time to get you to bed."

"Now thas what I'm talkin' about," Adeline slurs, running her tongue up his neck as he starts down the hall.

His deep voice rumbles something back, but we don't hear what he says.

Cam looks at me, grinning as I sway. "I see you ladies enjoyed the wine tonight."

Strutting over, I kiss his chest. "Of course. Now quick, before Adeline comes back for the game, naked Twister sounds like a great idea."

He chuckles. "I think we should leave the game." Holding me close, he rests his chin on my head and asks Elise, "Do you need any help cleaning up?"

She shakes her head. "Nah, get her home. I've got this."

I hug Elise before following Cam down the hall, slipping on my shoes.

Skipping outside, I turn and throw myself into Cam's arms. "I'm gonna climb you like a tree when we get home."

He chuckles, kissing my forehead before opening the car door for me.

"Seems like you all had fun." He holds my hand as he drives me home, all the warmth from his grasp flowing through me.

My heart feels so full having him back in my life. I want us to be what we were.

"What do you think about moving in? I have the room, and you never really unpacked much in the apartment at the clinic." The words spill out, but I'm glad. I want to be more vocal about the things I'm feeling and I know Cam needs to be included in that.

He squeezes my hand before pulling it away and turning onto my driveway. Once he parks, he turns to me. "Rae, I don't think that's a good idea. At least not yet."

My heart sinks, and my head starts spinning. "I see."

"Rae—"

"No, it's fine. But I think I'm going to go in alone. Raincheck on climbing you like a tree?" I give him a small smile as I open the door.

He gets out of the car, coming around to pull me into his arms. "I don't want you and wine to make this decision. I just want you to. We're headed there, but we need to sit down and talk about it first."

Nodding into his chest, I still feel the sting of his rejection. "Okay. We can talk about it later."

Lifting onto my toes, I kiss him and wish him a good night.

"Goodnight, Rae, I will see you tomorrow." His words barely register, but I nod.

In the house, I scoop Mocha up and take her to my room, sinking onto the bed. This is what happens when wine lowers my inhibitions. Now I have to face him and his rejection tomorrow.

CHAPTER
Twenty-Four

RAELYNN

Light shines through my open window right onto my face. "Ugh."

Yanking the blanket over my face, I try to go back to sleep, but the doorbell rings. And then rings again.

"Okay, okay." Rolling out of bed, I don't bother taking off my bonnet because I know who is at my door.

I open the door and turn without greeting Cam.

He chuckles. "Don't you want the coffee I brought for you?"

Turning back, I take the offered cup and grunt out a "thanks."

Cam follows me into the kitchen, where I take two ibuprofen and chug them down with the hot coffee. "I don't know how Elise managed to get her ass up and to Perk Up this morning. She drank more than I did."

"Yeah, but wine always tends to hit you harder than anything else." Cam sits at my kitchen table, sliding a bag across the table.

Sinking onto the chair opposite from him, I sigh. "Thank you. I didn't expect you to be here so early."

"It's eleven, Rae. I was going to come a couple hours ago but decided against it." He grins as I open the bag and find one of Elise's breakfast sandwiches.

Groaning as I take a bite, I meet Cam's amused gaze. "It's still warm."

He watches me polish off the sandwich and coffee, getting up and filling glasses with water for us both.

"Now that you have food and coffee in your belly, we need to talk about last night." His tone is cautious, but he continues, "I want you to know that I do want to live with you again, eventually, but we haven't even talked about all the things that kept us apart since the cabin. Sure, we scratched the surface, but we can't blow past it."

I lick my lips and sigh. "You're right, I know you're right. It's just hard. It's this weird feeling of restarting but everything is so familiar, it's hard not to want to go back to the way we were and forget it all. Make up for lost time."

"I know, but before we can do that, we should talk about what caused the end because I'm still a little unclear about what drove the decision. I mean, I understand you were trying to shield me, but it doesn't make sense why." He leans back in his chair, waiting.

Biting back my disappointment, I nod. It's reasonable to want to talk things through more. I don't want to relive the same mistakes. "For as long as I've known you, I've been aware that you want to be a dad. When month after month I was not able to give you that it broke my heart. Seeing your disappointment every time we had a negative result or my cycle started killed me. On top of that, I had to manage my own devastation. I tried to share with you how I was feeling, but as time went on, it felt like you were pulling away, spending less time with me and more time on other things."

He straightens, brows pinched together. "I wasn't pulling away. It felt like all we ever talked about was the baby and our lives revolved around it. Sometimes I just needed a break to know that there were other things than trying to get pregnant."

His voice is gentle, but I can hear the frustration.

"I wish I had known how you were feeling, because to me, it felt like you were closing off to disappointment. After the doctor told us it would be unlikely I would be able to conceive, the look on your face was completely shut down. I kept trying, hoping it would happen, and that day, as I was facing another disappointment, I realized I couldn't do it anymore. It was bad enough to break my own heart, but I couldn't handle not giving you what you always wanted."

My chest feels heavy as the weight of that reality still sits over me. Even though he said he's okay with not having kids, I need to be absolutely sure.

Cameron breathes out a heavy sigh. "I tried to talk to you, Rae. I looked like that because I could see how upset you were by the news and I didn't want you to see that I was okay with it because I didn't want to hurt you. But

Rae, don't you remember me telling you that I wanted to pull back from trying?"

Thinking back, I vaguely recall him trying to broach the subject. "Kind of. I think at the time I told myself you were just saying what you thought I wanted to hear."

"When have I ever done that? In the entirety of our relationship, I've always been honest with you." His exasperation rubs me the wrong way.

Defensive, I snap, "Do you think I was in any way mentally capable of seeing that? I was a goddamn mess. Maybe I didn't realize it then, but I can see it now. Nothing about my decision making back then is remotely close to what I would do now. I wish I could take it back, but I can't."

"I know, Rae Rae. I know." He softens.

Taking a deep breath, I continue to hold his gaze. "In the moment, I had myself convinced it was the only option. I know better now, and I will never make the mistake of thinking I know better without talking it out first. I have spent five years regretting a rash decision. I refuse to ever do that again."

He nods, silence filling the air between us. Cam releases a heavy breath, leaning forward and resting his elbows on the table. "I can see where you thought you needed to shield me. Looking back, I understand where I went wrong in how I attempted to cope and even how I tried to communicate. I think I shut you out too without realizing it because I thought you seemed to be doing okay as time went on. Now I know I missed so many signs."

Reaching across the table, I hold my hand out for his, squeezing when he takes it. "We were both coping as best as we knew how. I got a little ahead of myself in suggesting that you move in. I have more work to do, and you're still getting settled back here after everything. I know we don't want to make the same mistakes as before."

He smiles at me, rubbing his thumb back and forth over my hand. "Why don't we revisit it in a few months? You have no idea how hard it is to say no to taking this step again. I want it as much as you, but I also need to know it's going to be forever."

It will be forever. I know it in my heart, but I also know that Cam needs to see the progress in my actions and not just conversations. Licking my lips, I give him a small smile. "I get it. We will get there."

I love you.

I know he feels it too, but neither of us can say the words out loud yet, and maybe that's a sign that I need to stop getting ahead of myself.

CHAPTER
Twenty-Five

RAELYNN

Adjusting my laptop as I shift to get comfortable, I think about the question Dr. Fletcher just asked. When I talked to Cam last week about my thought process that led to our end, I never once addressed the fact that having biological children will likely not happen for us.

Closing my eyes, I take a couple deep breaths. "I never thought about why I didn't bring it up in the present, but I think I'm scared. I'm worried that even though he said in passing that he doesn't want children with anyone else, one day he will wake up full of regret."

"That can be daunting, but I think you need a real answer in order to move forward as a couple but also in coming to terms with your grief and the reality of what this means for your relationship." She jots a couple notes down before closing her book. "I want you to talk to Cam about it. I think it's an important conversation for your healing and his."

I nod. "Okay." We say goodbye, and I close my laptop, lean back on my couch, and close my eyes. She's right, it is an important conversation, but it's one I'm scared to have.

Needing a coffee after the session, I head to Perk Up. Elise looks up from the book she's reading and grins.

"Oh my goodness, I don't know what's going on, but it's been dead all day." She works on making me a latte as I lean against the counter. "I've already deep cleaned the kitchen and prepped everything I need for tomorrow."

"Now that I think about it, everywhere I've gone, it's been quiet. I think it's just so nice outside that people are taking advantage." Taking the latte she hands me, I glance at the time. "Actually, can you also make a mocha for Cam? I think I'm going to pop by to see him."

Elise grins as she works on my request. "I'm so glad things are going well with you two. It's nice to see you so happy."

"I am happy. I do need to talk to him about whether or not having children is a deal breaker. We kind of touched on it but never really went anywhere with the conversation." Paying, I take the second drink.

"That must be nerve-racking. How are you feeling about that talk?" She leans onto the counter, eyes on me.

Chewing on my lower lip, I tug on a curl. "Nervous. It's like this ghost that still lingers in our relationship. So even though I don't think he would be back here, working on things with me if he wasn't okay with it, the conversation is so overdue that it's daunting."

Elise nods. "That makes sense. When you've put something off for too long, it becomes bigger."

"Exactly. But I can't put it off any longer."

"Well, good luck. Maybe I will close up early and bring some food to Adeline and Brynne at the shelter. If everyone is enjoying the beautiful day, I can take advantage of it too."

Grinning, I nod approvingly. "Good. Text me later and we can go for a walk or something."

She locks up behind me, waving through the door before flipping the sign.

I head to the clinic, my heart beating heavily in my chest as I drive.

Cam mentioned he had a clear afternoon, so he was spending the time going through files and getting things organized more to his liking. Business has been steady since the town realized there's no drama, and he's finally feeling settled enough to tweak some things.

The bell rings as I enter the clinic. It's quiet, all the staff gone for the day.

Cam comes out looking annoyed, but he smiles when he sees me and the cup I'm holding.

"Hey! What a nice surprise. Just in time, my head is spinning from all the files I've been going through." He kisses me before taking the coffee and leading me to his office.

Settling into one of the chairs, I sip at my latte and watch in amusement as he tries to clear a space on his desk.

"I needed something after counseling and missed you. I don't need to stay long, it looks like you still have a ton to get through." Gesturing at the stack of boxes next to his desk, along with piles of paper strewn across half the room, I chuckle.

"No, please, stay. Everything is starting to bleed together." He runs his hand over his head. "Suzanne had a system that clearly worked for her, but even after she and Penelope went over it, I still don't know how she could keep track of it all."

Scrunching my nose, I look around with empathy. I can see how this would be a challenging part of taking over a business.

Licking my lips, I debate whether now is the time to talk to him about kids, but to hell with it. "So, I wanted to talk to you about something that came up in counseling today."

"Okay." His expression is open, comforting.

Blowing out my breath, I rub my palms over my knees. "We never really talked about how my infertility will impact our future. I know you talked about it in relation to the end of your marriage to Sarah, but the likelihood that we can have children is so low that I want to see if this is a deal breaker. Are you okay if we never conceive?"

Cam comes around the table, kneeling on the ground in front of me. "Raelynn, I don't need children when I have you. I love you. I've always loved you, and nothing can change that."

Wrapping my arms around him, I brush my lips over his. "I love you too. You're one hundred percent sure?"

He chuckles. "Absolutely. Besides, down the line if we decide we want kids, there are other options. We could consider surrogacy or adoption. But that's only if we choose it's what we want together, and it feels right."

"That's something that has been on my mind, but right now, I want to focus on us and nothing else."

Grinning, he says, "I'm on board with that."

Eyeing the desk, I smirk. "How attached are you to the papers on your desk?"

He shakes his head. "I haven't even had time to sort them. Why?"

Standing, I push the papers onto the floor before crooking my finger at him.

Cam groans, closing the distance between us and lifting me onto his desk as his lips crash against mine.

He pulls back to pull his shirt over his head before removing mine and tossing it out of the way. He kisses his way down my body, stripping me down before stroking me with his tongue.

"As much as I want to spend more time here..." He runs a finger through my wetness, "I am expecting Penelope back this afternoon, limiting our time."

My heart pounds as he strips the rest of the way, working his cock before pulling me to the edge of the desk. He slides in, groaning before he moves faster.

"Harder," I moan.

His tongue strokes mine as we move, my entire body electric. Our sex life has never been lacking, but this feels different, like a weight or pressure has been lifted. The pressure of knowing our relationship would be missing something. But I can see now what I couldn't see then, all Cam wants is me and our happiness together. Everything else is extra.

It doesn't take long for my orgasm to hit. My head falls back as my body pulses in pleasure. Cam moans as he comes, his forehead dropping to my shoulder. We stay like this, our breathing heavy and pure bliss fills me.

"I—"

Before I can finish, the sound of the bell jingling from the front spurs us into action.

Cam shuts the door, locking it as Penelope calls out a greeting.

We cover our mouths as we snicker, tossing clothes as we struggle to dress.

"Oh my god. She's going to know what we did." I cover my face and chuckle.

Cam laughs, picking papers up off the floor and spreading them on his desk. As I settle in the chair, he hands me my latte.

When he opens the door, greeting Penelope like nothing happened, I barely hold it together.

She smiles at me when she comes inside. "Hey, Raelynn. Did you come to help Cam?"

Swallowing hard, I don't meet Cam's gaze. "Yeah, I thought he needed a little incentive to keep working. I brought him some caffeine."

I quickly grab my things. "I will let you get to it. Cam, I will have dessert waiting at my house later."

His eyes burn into me as I wave and rush out the door.

CHAPTER
Twenty-Six

CAMERON

The door to Young Jae's house opens, and a delicious scent of whatever he's cooking greets me. "Hey! Owen is running behind, which works out because I got home late, so I'm still cooking. How was your day?"

I follow him into the kitchen, handing him a beer and putting the rest of the case in the fridge. "It was busy. Ari found a dog that was thrown out of a vehicle and brought it into the clinic. No chip or tattoo. Clearly starving, but thankfully, nothing was broken. I will fix her up and then see if Brynne can find her a space at the shelter."

"Damn, that's awful. I don't understand how someone could do that to an animal." Young Jae plates the pork belly he's made, along with some rice, gochujang, and lettuce and sets it all on the table as Owen comes in the door.

Sitting down, I say, "It's a cute Jack Russell. So, if you know anyone looking, let me know. Maybe she won't need to go to the shelter."

Owen comes in, catching the end of the conversation. "Shelter? They're pretty full right now. Brynne was hoping to use some of the money raised at the masquerade ball to work on expanding the space, but they had to do some pretty major repairs to the existing space, so there's not enough money left. They have a marginal budget for advertising, Adeline said she spoke to Rae about needing some graphics made."

Kicking out a chair for Owen, I grin. "Rae mentioned. She's excited for the chance."

We dig in, wrapping the rice, pork belly, and gochujang into the lettuce. Whenever Young Jae hosts our get-togethers, he always cooks a delicious Korean dish. But this one is a crowd favorite.

"You know, Elise has always wanted a Jack Russell. Once she's all fixed up, let me know," Young Jae throws out casually.

Glancing at Owen, we raise our brows. "I thought Jake didn't want a dog?"

Young Jae scowls. "Right. Well, the dog can stay here then, and she can visit it any time."

None of us like her boyfriend. He's never made an effort to get to know any of Elise's friends, and from what Adeline has told me, he's always on his phone doing nothing and spends very little time with Elise.

We don't need to say anything to know we're all thinking the same thing, but she needs to decide what she's willing to put up with.

"Once she's well enough, you can come and meet her. She's sweet, but I want to run more tests to make sure we didn't miss anything. She's negative for parvo, but I still have her isolated until I run a few more tests." Young Jae nods, his expression giving little away as to what he's thinking.

He works from home as a highly sought after architect, so a dog might be good company, but I never thought of him as having a pet.

After dinner, we clear the table to play poker.

Owen smiles when his phone beeps with a text.

"How are you enjoying living with Adeline?" I ask, smirking as he answers her message, the goofy grin never falling from his face.

He leans back in his chair. "It's better than I could've ever imagined. When are you and Raelynn moving back in?"

I shrug. "I don't know. She asked, but there were some things we still needed to talk about. Now I'm wondering why I told her we would revisit it in a few months. I feel like we've talked everything through enough that I'm confident we can work through anything that comes up, but I guess I'm a little hesitant since I thought we were solid before."

It's hard to fully let go of what happened, despite how happy I am with Rae. I can see how hard she is working on showing things will be different, and we've had some hard conversations. It's hard to feel like I'm doubting her when I know she's doing her best.

Young Jae stands, grabbing another round of beer. "I get it, man. But you didn't see her afterward. For a bit, she seemed to be doing okay. Then she went away for a week-end, no one really knows where, and when she came back, it was clear she knew she made a mistake. Then she saw pictures of you and Sarah and jumped to the conclusion we all did."

"Yeah, I don't know the extent of it, but she was making choices that we all worried about since they seemed unsafe, and James eventually sat her down. I don't know what he said, but she seemed to be a bit better after that. Something was missing though, she tried to hide it, but we could all see she wasn't happy. Not in the way we all know her to be," Owen chimes in.

It hurts to know how much she was suffering, and I don't ask about what she was doing that James felt he needed to intervene on because I have the feeling I wouldn't be happy with the answer. It's likely not some-thing anyone but Raelynn should share.

"I hear what you're saying. I will see how it goes."

They nod, turning their attention more to the game. As I fold, I wonder what is holding me back. I know Raelynn is the one I want to be with. What is making me want to stay where we're at instead of moving forward?

CHAPTER
Twenty-Seven

RAELYNN

Holding my breath, I click the link with the grade for my first exam.

A.

Squealing, I jump up and dance around the room. "Mocha! I got an A!"

She peeks at me from under the chair, meowing and judging me.

My phone rings, so I laugh and say, "Saved by the bell, Mocha!"

Seeing Elise's name, I swipe and say hello in a singsong voice.

"Raelynn..." Elise's voice is serious, the tone making my blood run cold.

Sitting on my chair, I absently start stroking Mocha's

hair when she hops on my lap. "Are you okay? What's wrong?"

"The chief's wife came in today and told me they got called into a precarious situation. You remember Brynne's family?" The distaste in her voice is palpable.

My heart sinks. Brynne's father and brothers are really horrid people who live about fifteen minutes out of town on a property that makes the state of Adeline's house when she moved in look like an oasis.

I'm positive they're doing illegal things, and any time there's a call out to their place, we're always on edge because it's escalated more than once to the point Brynne's older brother is still in jail.

That property is not a safe place for any cop, least of all James. He was the one who arrested and testified against the eldest Hart child, Colton. I don't know how Brynne came out of there somewhat normal, it must have been her mom's influence. The mouse of a woman never says a word and is always jumpy, but she's not like the rest. She is kind.

"Shit."

"She said it's all-hands-on-deck, and they were called out over an hour ago." Elise's voice is soft as she delivers the blow.

My heart sinks. The Hart family is volatile and if they're all going out there, the situation is not good. "Thank you for letting me know."

We say goodbye, leaving me staring into space. Mocha crawls up to rub her face onto mine, so I soak in her purrs and try not to imagine the worst.

Jumping when my phone rings again, I don't check the

screen before I answer, "Yes?!"

Slumping back when Cam's voice greets me, I get up and pace. "Is everything okay, Rae?" he asks.

"I don't know. Elise called and said all the cops got called to the Hart's place. James is the cop who arrested and ultimately got Colton sentenced to prison, so I'm worried. They're volatile on a good day." My voice wavers despite my effort to keep it steady.

"Shit, I remember hearing about that. What can I do?" Even though my gut instinct is to ask him to come over, I know he has an incredibly busy day today and don't want to add to his plate.

Pacing into the living room, I stare out the window to my backyard. "Nothing. I won't be good company until I know he's okay."

"Rae, what do you need? You made a promise. Please keep it," he chides me gently.

My voice is a whisper, guilt surging through me. "If it works, I would rather not be alone."

"I can make it work. See you soon."

We say goodbye, and I lay on the couch, scrolling the town's social media site for any news, but there is nothing.

Cam comes in twenty minutes later, finding me still prone on the couch, trying to find any news. He sits at my feet, rubbing them as I toss my phone onto the coffee table and growl.

"Elise said they have been out there for over an hour. How is there no news about what's going on?" I'm ready to crawl out of my skin, but nothing can make me feel better in this moment.

"I know it's hard, but they're well trained, and we will

hear from James as soon as he can reach out. You know he always tells you he's safe when there's ever been any situation where something could've happened." His hands keep working on my feet, slowly helping me relax a little.

Giving him an apologetic look, I murmur, "Thank you for coming. I think I would've gone crazy alone."

He pulls me onto his lap, hugging me close. "Any time you need me, I'm here."

We cuddle close for a while before I remember how my day started. "I did have some good news today. I got an A on my exam."

Cam pulls back, his face shining with pride. "I never doubted it! We should talk about some things I could use your help with at the clinic. I would pay you, of course."

Beaming at him, I almost forget why he's sitting on my couch when the phone rings.

He reaches across, grabbing it for me, but before I can answer, my front door opens.

"Rae Rae?" James's voice calls down the hallway.

I fall off Cam's lap in my hurry to get to my brother. Throwing myself into him when I see he's okay, I hold him tight.

"I know you love your job, but damn, I hate knowing you put yourself at risk every day." Dropping my arms, I step back to really examine him. His eyes are strained, but there's not a scuff on his body or hair out of place.

He nods at Cam when he sees him before turning back to me. "It's Willowbrook Lake, Rae, shit rarely hits the fan here."

"So what happened?" Now that I know he's okay, curiosity burns.

He plops down on my couch, shaking his head as he grins. "So nosy."

"C'mon," I whine, knowing he will give in.

Rolling his eyes, he gives me and Cam firm looks. "This stays here, got it?"

We both nod.

"Colton got released on parole two days ago, and one of the stipulations is he has to stay within a certain zone, and he left that zone by going to the Hart cabin. We got a tip that he was there and went in." He smirks. "He had a chance to be free and lost it real quick."

Shaking my head, I drop down on the couch between him and Cam. "Damn, that could've been bad."

"It's why we all went. Man was wasted. They all were except Mrs. Hart. That woman, I don't think she's the same as the rest, but she will never leave. I remember Brynne trying to get her out, but she gave up." James shakes his head, his mouth dropping.

We've all seen how the Hart men treat Mrs. Hart.

"Do you want me to stay a while?" Cam asks me. Glancing at the time, I know he needs to get back to work.

"I'm okay now that I know James is in one piece."

Cam stands, bending down to give me a kiss. He claps James on the shoulder after he pulls away. "Glad you're okay. Rae, I need to get back to the clinic, but I will call you later."

James grins at me as Cam shuts the front door, leaving us alone. "Maybe I should've knocked first."

Smacking him, I press my hand to my chest. "Excuse me, I was worried about you not thinking about that!"

He tilts his head back, closing his eyes. I get up and grab him some water before settling in next to him.

"I'm glad to see you so happy, Rae." He rolls his head to look at me, giving me a small smile. "But I miss our weekly dinners. You've been busy with work, and Cam, now adding school into the mix. I get it, but I miss you."

Scooching over, I lean into him and lay my head on his shoulder. "I know, I'm sorry. I've had a bit of tunnel vision lately. I will do better, I promise. Why don't you go home, clean up, and then come over and I will make that green curry soup you really like."

"That sounds amazing." He gives me a squeeze before excusing himself.

As he leaves, I send Cam a text to raincheck on tonight, explaining I have been neglecting my relationship with James and want to spend the evening with him.

> Of course. I never even thought about that with how much time we've been spending together. Tomorrow?

> Sounds perfect. Thank you <3

———

The door opens a few hours later as I finish setting the table and getting the final touches of dinner ready.

Along with the soup, I made Thai basil beef rolls, and a Thai cucumber salad. My mouth has been watering all afternoon while I prepped and cooked.

"Damn, sis. I thought you were making soup." He

stares at the food covering my small table, shaking his head.

Laughing, I sit down. "I had to make it up to you. Dig in!"

We serve ourselves as I catch him up on my schooling, his enthusiasm for my A almost matching my own.

James groans as he bites into a roll. "Oh my god. This is so good."

Smiling, I say, "Thank you."

"So, how's it going with Cam? I assume well since you seem happy and super busy these days." His expression would be fierce if his eyes weren't twinkling with humor.

I shrug. "Good. We're talking about things in ways we never did before, and I appreciate seeing that growth in us personally as well as in our relationship. I want to know we're progressing though. It's not like a new relationship. We already know basically everything important about the other, minus some gaps from the past five years. So I don't want to go at the pace a brand new relationship would. But I feel hesitancy from him, and that makes me nervous."

He sets his spoon down and assesses me.

Squirming, I scowl. "You know I hate when you do that. Your 'work' stare."

He smirks. "I'm gauging how receptive you will be to what I want to say."

"When has that stopped you before?" I shoot back.

"True." He shrugs and continues. "You need to understand from his perspective that your relationship was solid before. Was it hard to go through trying to conceive and having no success? Of course, but in his mind, that was the hard part, not your relationship. So when you ended things, it swept the rug out from under him. He's trying to protect himself from that happening again. That man loves you. I believe he came back here for you. But a part of him doesn't fully trust you and your commitment to each other yet."

It hurts. The truth in James's words are what I haven't been able to see, and knowing what he's saying is valid pains me.

He sighs, opening his mouth to say something, but I hold up my hand and shake my head. "No, you're right. I need to rebuild his trust."

We change the subject to other things, like my career transition plan. And soon all the food is gone, nothing left over.

James helps me clear the table, refusing to let me clean up the kitchen, so I relax on the couch with Mocha until he finishes.

"What about you? Anyone special in your life?"

He scoffs. "Nah. I know too much about everyone in this town, so unless someone new moves here, I will just focus on building myself a life I love."

Shaking my head, I grin. "You never know. One day, someone you never considered before may catch your attention. We also have been growing a lot as a town. You could meet someone new too."

He just rolls his eyes and changes the subject to our

parents. James has always kept his private life separate from everything. He's dated here and there, but I can't recall anyone serious.

It makes me sad because I know the type of man my brother is, and he deserves someone amazing.

CHAPTER
Twenty~Eight

RAELYNN

Cam hugs me closer when I try to crawl out of bed. "Not yet. Five more minutes of cuddling." His raspy voice makes me want to stay in bed for longer than five minutes, but I was an idiot who booked an early morning showing.

"That's what you said five minutes ago." Kissing his chest, I slide down and roll off the bed. "I have that showing this morning and then classes this afternoon."

He groans, sitting up and glancing at the time. "Being an adult with responsibilities sucks."

Chuckling, I start grabbing some clothes. "You're just upset there's no time for morning sex."

He grins at me shamelessly as I get dressed. "I see nothing wrong with that."

Cam hops out of bed, throws on some sweats, and

heads out the bedroom door with a promise to have breakfast ready for me shortly.

Taking off my bonnet, I cringe at the mess of my curls. I spritz it with a new hydrating mist I picked up from Tamarya's and get to work on sections. Moving as quickly as I can, it still takes more time than I have to get them looking satisfactory before I rush to the table for a hurried breakfast with Cam.

We eat quickly together, sorting out plans for the evening. I wish we could do this every day, but I'm not going to push Cam toward something he's not ready for.

The day blurs by. The buyer finally finds a house she likes and puts in an offer. The market in Willowbrook Lake is a bit odd, but thankfully, a few towns in the surrounding areas are pushing for more growth.

I'm not even upset at how hard the town works to stay small, the vibes are amazing and it doesn't get too busy in the summer.

I'm exhausted when I get to Cam's for dinner. It took hours to finish my class project, and I still feel like something isn't quite right.

"You look like you could use this." Cam hands me a glass of wine as I walk into his kitchen. "Dinner is already on the table."

Sipping, I sigh. "Thank you. I submitted a big project but I can't shake the feeling that it's not going to do well."

He comes over, kissing me. "You never know, but if you're right, then I know you will take the feedback and learn from it."

Sitting in the seat he pulls out for me, I relax. "That's true."

Dinner is delicious and another reminder of how easy things always were with Cam. I never need to fight for things to say when I'm with him.

"How is counseling going?" He pushes his plate back.

"Good. I feel like we've worked through a lot, and Dr. Fletcher seems to agree because she wants to meet monthly instead of biweekly now." I stand and start clearing the table. "I really appreciate her style because I saw my previous counselor for close to three years, and while it was nice talking to her, I feel like I've gained so much more this time."

Cam comes and wraps his arms around me. "I'm glad. Want to tell me about it?"

Leaning into him, I soak in his warmth. "She's been helping me identify my triggers so I can stay on top of them, like when my period is late. We've gone over grounding and coping exercises."

"That sounds helpful. Does it feel like it will be manageable in the moment?"

Turning in his arms, I rest my chin on his chest and look up. "It does, but it's hard to say what will happen in the moment. But we've also been talking about communication and how to rebuild that trust between us from when it was lost."

His gaze is soft as he takes me in, before he brushes his lips against mine. "I love you."

"Love you too." Wrapping my arms around his neck, I kiss him deeply. "Should we skip the dishes and go to your bedroom?"

He lifts me, grinning. "I love how you think."

CHAPTER
Twenty~Nine

CAMERON

The bell to the clinic rings. It's been a quiet day, so I sent Penelope home. Ashton heads to the front, nodding as I thank him. He's quiet but works hard. Maybe I need to plan something with the staff to get to know them on a more personal level. Now that I feel like I have my footing and business is staying steady.

"They're in examination room one, doc." He heads back to where he's running some tests and charting for me.

Grabbing the folder, I pause when I see the name. Elaine Simmons.

The Simmons own the Victorian that Rae has dreamt of living in her entire life. My parents are good friends with the Simmons, and Rae fell in love with the house when she joined us there for a Christmas party.

I reached out to them six years ago to see if they were

interested in selling since they spend well over six months of the year traveling, but at the time, their son still lived at home, and they weren't prepared to sell. My parents told me their son moved out a couple years later, at the time I was relieved I hadn't been able to buy the house.

Opening the door, I greet Mrs. Simmons warmly. "Good afternoon, Mrs. Simmons. It's been a long time. How are you and Mr. Simmons?"

She smiles, cradling a small Yorkshire Terrier. "We're good. We came back to town to settle some business. Daisy seemed out of sorts on the plane, which is unusual, so I wanted to make sure she's okay."

Putting on my stethoscope, I listen to her heart. Mrs. Simmons holds her gently on the table as I go through the preliminary checks. "I hope everything is okay and the business isn't too serious."

"Well, we've decided it's time to sell the house. It's the other reason I came here. I heard that you and Miss Gaetz are together again. I was overjoyed to hear that, as I have always admired your love for one another. I wanted to see if you were still interested in the house. We don't really want people traipsing through it, and I would love to see the home go to someone I know who will love it as much as our family does."

My hands pause from checking Daisy's joint movement. "Yes. I am absolutely interested."

"Good, please come and see it. We've done some upgrades, and I want you to be sure." Her voice is firm.

"Of course, but you know we love the house, and I doubt anything would change our minds." I continue to check Daisy over calmly when I feel anything but calm inside.

"I still want you to come see it. But since you're confident, I will send over a proposal we have already drafted, just in case. Review it and let me know if any tweaks need to be made. We can sign after you've viewed the house."

Excitement races through me as I think about how happy this will make Raelynn. "That sounds great. Let me know when I can come by."

I can't stop the smile that forms, biting it back when Daisy gives a little yelp as I check her front left side.

"Good news is, it's nothing serious. Considering her age, she probably has arthritis in the front left shoulder, which is quite common in these little dogs. Especially if she hops up and down on furniture, the impact can cause wear and tear. Let's start there with treatment. I will get some material on things you can do. It seems early since you said she's been good so far, so I recommend a joint supplement along with reducing any big jumps. If it doesn't improve, we can look at other options, but that would involve more invasive testing, which we want to avoid if we can."

"I will do whatever I need to." Mrs. Simmons comforts Daisy as I excuse myself.

"Penelope, can you please grab some joint supplements and an anti-inflammatory for Daisy?" I write down the dosage on my chart and hand it to her before grabbing the information on arthritis in dogs.

"Of course, Dr. Hall." She takes the charts and heads to the front.

Rejoining Mrs. Simmons in the room, I provide her the

pamphlets and go over the medications I'm recommend-
ing. "The anti-inflammatory is meant for an as needed
basis. You can give her some over the next four weeks as
she is in pain, and after four weeks you should revisit it
with a vet. I want you to use the joint supplement daily as
it will help prevent further damage. I cannot stress
enough, please don't let her jump down off furniture."

"Of course, thank you." Mrs. Simmons gently places
Daisy back in her carrier. "I will send over the contract.
Look at it and let us know when you want to see the
house."

She reaches out, giving me an affectionate squeeze on
my forearm.

"I will check my schedule and let you know. Thank you
for trusting me with your home. I promise we will cherish
the memories we make in it."

Following her out of the room, we say goodbye before I
hand my notes to Ashton and head into my office. Shutting
the door, I pump my fist.

I can't wait to tell Raelynn, but I want to finalize the
details first.

Picking up my phone, I call Owen. "You will never
believe what just happened."

———

Owen parks next to me in front of the Simmons' home. It's
been two days since Mrs. Simmons offered to sell it to me.
It's been close to ten years since I've been inside the home,
so I solicited Owen's help to look over the house as I
review the agreement.

Excitement surges through me as Mr. Simmons opens the door. "Good morning. Come on in."

We follow him in, the entrance of the home as grand and welcoming as I remember. It's in immaculate condition, considering how often it's empty.

Owen excuses himself to look around with Mr. Simmons's permission as I follow him into the front sitting room.

"I am so thrilled that you are entrusting me with your family home." Sitting across from Mr. and Mrs. Simmons, I take the paperwork they've drafted. They've been very reasonable with quick possession once financing goes through. Offers to provide all documentation on any repairs done around the house, including upgrades. Then I get to the amount they're asking for and pause. "I think the figure for the sale amount is wrong."

Handing the page back to them, my knee jiggles as they look.

"No, this is correct." Mrs. Simmons looks at me quizzically as she hands it back.

Taking a deep breath, I push on as politely as possible. "It's just, it seems a little—low. Are you sure?"

Mr. Simmons gives me a stern look, one that reminds me of my father. "Son, we are certain. It's why we wrote it down. You're saving us costs and we know how much Raelynn loves this house. That's all we want, for it to go to someone who will love it as much as we have."

Smiling, I say, "Well, okay then." And sign the contract. I was a little worried about financing prior to seeing the number, but now I know I will be okay. "I have an appointment at the bank this afternoon. I will keep you posted."

They suggest I find Owen and I join him in exploring the house. It's as beautiful as I remember with four bedrooms upstairs, three and a half bathrooms, an office, sitting room, family room, dining room, and spacious kitchen all on the main floor. The space I remember Rae loving the most is the third floor. The attic is cozy. The deeply angled ceilings and one round turret were all she could talk about after seeing it. She used to dream about all the things she could do in the room. The basement has been finished with a wet bar, home entertainment space, and another bedroom and bathroom.

We tour around, Owen checking everything thoroughly, but there's nothing that stands out as a concern.

Back in the car with Owen, he turns and grins at me. "You're getting a steal of a deal, man. There is not a damn thing wrong in that house. Unless you and Rae decide you want to update anything aesthetically, it's move in ready."

Breathing a sigh of relief, I smile. "That's amazing news. I can't wait to surprise Rae."

CHAPTER
Thirty

RAELYNN

Cam's voice calls for me as I run some curl cream through my hair, working it through until I'm happy with the results. "I'm almost done!"

He enters the bathroom, the corners of his eyes crinkling when he sees me. "You look beautiful."

Stepping into his arms, I lift up to kiss him. "I'm glad you appreciate the effort."

He chuckles. "Ready to go? Somehow even in a town this small, I haven't run into your parents. I'm a little nervous to see them again."

"You know Dad never leaves the farm. And Mom is so busy with her women's group and whatever else she's got going around town, it's not surprising. But don't be nervous. They're looking forward to seeing you." He kisses me on my forehead before crouching down to scoop up Mocha.

My heart is full as I watch him coo at her and she soaks it up before we feed her and head out.

Cam drives, one hand on the steering wheel, his other resting on the gear shift. He's relaxed, his mouth in a soft smile. He's had the look he can't hide when he has some surprise on his face since he walked in the door, but I know he won't budge until he's ready to tell me.

Watching him, I recall all the times we've made this drive, from when we were teenagers until shortly before our relationship ended.

He has always adored going to the family farm, often helping my dad when needed. Or joking around with Mom as she attempted to teach him some Jamaican dishes. Then she would tease him because she said he could never get the spice quite right.

He gives me a sidelong glance. "What's so funny over there?"

"I remember when Momma tried to teach you how to cook Pepper Pot Soup and she was teasing you because you couldn't get the flavor to her liking." Laughing, I gasp out, "And the time she showed you her recipe for Jerk chicken. She thought you forgot to season the chicken."

Cam laughs. "It took me years to live that one down."

Reaching over, I squeeze his hand. "She has always loved that you have such a good sense of humor."

"Your mom knows the difference between teasing in fun and teasing to be mean. She's always fun." Cam's voice is affectionate.

His fingers tap on the steering wheel as we turn into my parents' driveway.

They're outside waiting for us as Cam pulls up, parking alongside Dad's truck.

As soon as Cam steps out of the car, Mom envelops him in a hug. "Welcome home."

Cam holds on tight for a moment before pulling away, his eyes widening when my dad also hugs him. He stares at me over Dad's shoulder as I cover my mouth to stop myself from laughing. "If you ever let her stubborn ass convince you to leave again, you will be in trouble."

"Not going to happen, sir," Cam promises.

Rolling my eyes, I throw my arms up. "I'm right here. Geez."

Momma laughs, linking her arm with mine. "Dinner's on the table. I made Cam's favorite."

"Jerk chicken?" Cam's eyes light up as he and Dad follow us into the house.

"With all the flavor," Momma teases, leading us to an overloaded table.

"Momma, how many people did you invite to dinner?" I sit down, eyeing the mounds of food.

She grins. "Just us, but I'm sending the leftovers home with Cam."

Laughing as Cam fist pumps the air, we dive into dinner. My heart is full as we chat, and it feels like life is coming together the way it was always supposed to.

"Did you hear about the Simmons' house?" Mom asks as she sets her fork and knife down.

Shaking my head, I lean forward, hope filling me that maybe they've finally decided to sell.

"They sold the house this week, didn't even get it to market. I saw Mrs. Simmons at the community center today. She wouldn't tell me who bought it, just said it was going to the people it was meant for." She shrugs, not fully understanding what her words are doing to me.

Cam's hand reaches under the table, squeezing mine.

Swallowing hard, I give Cam's hand a light squeeze back before standing to help clean up. "I'm sure they're excited for this new chapter."

Mom follows me into the kitchen as I start washing dishes. "What's wrong?"

Scrubbing at the dish, I shake my head. "It's stupid."

She rests her hand on my arm, stopping me. "No, it's not."

"I always had this picture of me and Cam living in that house one day. Even if that picture no longer includes children, I still saw us in that home. Creating memories. Maybe even adapting some of the space for you and Dad when you're ready to travel more." Slumping against the counter, I sigh. "I know that having Cam back is enough. And we don't need the space. That house has been my dream, and it feels like another piece of the life I wanted has just slipped away."

Turning as she pulls me into her arms, I rest my head on her shoulder. "Baby girl, life has a funny way of working out sometimes. The road you and Cam have traveled to get here hasn't been easy, but everything will work out. I promise."

Soaking in her warmth, I focus on the way life has been going well. Taking a deep breath, I pull away. "Okay, Momma, I will try not to dwell."

We head back to sit at the table where Cam and my dad are talking, and I catch the tail end of their conversation. "I'm definitely sure." Cam's eyes are on me as he says that.

"Sure about what?" I narrow my eyes, scanning between them.

Cam reaches his hand out for mine, stroking his thumb over the delicate skin. "You. Definitely you. And us. I've never been more sure about us."

Warmth flows through me as I bend to kiss him and I realize the house doesn't matter. All that matters is this.

CHAPTER
Thirty-One

RAELYNN

The next few days Cameron is really busy, which works out because I have a ton of assignments due. Despite my doubts, my last assignment received an A, which helped me gain some confidence in my skills.

As I turn in my final assignment, I pull up an email from my professor.

Raelynn,

I wanted to reach out to you personally. I've been really impressed with the quality of your work. I have a friend in the industry who will occasionally take on students for paid work experience.

I showed her some of your projects, and she would love to connect with you if you're interested. Let me know either way.

. . .

T. Rush

Gaping at my screen, I type out a response expressing my interest. I've been feeling the pinch from reducing my clients and listings to make school work, so something to help fill that gap and add to my resume is better than I expected.

She responds quickly with the contact information.

Opening a new email, I type out my expression of interest and send it off. As soon as the email is sent, I question its phrasing and wonder if it came across the way I intended.

Giving myself a shake, I close my email. "No, Raelynn Gaetz. This negative self-talk shit has to stop. It's not you."

It's something that has reared its ugly head with all the changes in my life, something Dr. Fletcher noticed and has started to address in counseling. I struggled with self-doubt a lot as a curly-haired, biracial girl. There was no one with hair like mine, food like mine, or skin like mine when I was in junior high. Momma helped me through a lot of it and as I grew older my confidence also grew.

In counseling, Dr. Fletcher said that making big life changes can often trigger those innate responses. It's something I've been trying to be more aware of.

Mocha meows at me from the door, drawing my attention from my computer. I glance at the time, gasping. "Oh, baby! I'm so sorry. You must be hungry."

Scooping her up, I carry her to her dish and mix some

wet food with the dry, giving her a little extra for being late for her dinner before I scrounge for something to eat.

There's a knock on the door before the beeping of the keyless system carries down the hall.

"Raelynn?" Cam's voice is followed by his footsteps as he comes into the kitchen. "I brought burgers if you're hungry."

"You're my hero." Grabbing a couple beers from the fridge, I kiss him before sitting down. "I have some news. My professor is really impressed by my work, so she referred me to a connection that hires students for paid work experience. I just sent my email expressing my interest."

"Babe! That's incredible news!" Cam hands me the meal he ordered for me but doesn't start eating.

"I don't have more info just yet, but I will let you know once I hear back." I shrug, wondering if he's waiting for me.

Cam clears his throat. "No, I, uh, well, I also have a surprise. But I want to tell you somewhere special. Can we take a drive tonight? Or do you have more homework to do?"

"I'm done my assignments. So wherever you want to go, let's go."

He starts eating, his brows furrowed. My nerves kick in as we finish our meal in silence, but not our normal silence. Something is distracting him and has been for almost a week now. I can't help but be taken back to when it felt like he was pulling away from me, but I shake it off. We made a promise to each other.

He cleans up after we eat, then takes my hand, and we head to the car.

Cam opens the car door for me, kissing me before I get in. "I promise it's a good surprise."

Smiling, I relax as he gets in and heads out. Before we get out of my neighborhood, he hands me a blindfold.

"Are we doing something kinky?" Smirking, I slip it on. "Are we parking, and you're going to ravish me?"

He laughs, driving for a while before we come to a stop. "No, not this time."

The car door opens and shuts before mine opens, and his hand is on my arm. Cam guides me over some concrete to a grassy spot, turning me until he's happy. He stands behind me, wrapping his arms around my waist.

"Take off the blindfold." His low voice in my ear sends shivers through me, my body aching for him.

Lifting the blindfold, I freeze when I see the Simmons' home in front of me. The white house is grand, standing three stories high with two turrets and a dormer. The main level has a covered wraparound porch that I've coveted ever since I was a little girl. Even more so after I got to attend their annual Christmas party with Cam and his parents.

The second floor has a patio that wraps around a third of the building. I've never seen it up close, but I suspect it's attached to the primary suite.

Everything about the house is pristine and looks like it's pulled straight from a fairytale. A knot forms in my throat, and I'm unsure why we're here.

"I bought it. For us."

It's like time stops. Everything is frozen as I process what he just told me.

Cam is the buyer. Cam bought the house. For us. To live in. I'm quivering as it sinks in that he made my dream house happen somehow. I don't think I've ever felt so stunned or excited in my entire life.

His arms fall from around me as I take it all in before spinning and gaping at him.

He smiles at me, adoration and love shining from his eyes. "It's why I've been so busy this week. I've been getting financing and everything in order. We can't rush some things because they take time, but the Simmons will be clearing out the house in the next couple of weeks and will provide keys for us then, regardless of whether all the paperwork has cleared."

Leaping into his arms, I pepper his face with kisses. "Oh my god. This is the most incredible surprise I would never have expected. I love you."

He laughs, spinning me in a circle. "It was so hard not to tell you at your parents, but I wanted to make sure it was a done deal."

Sighing, I look back at the house and my heart feels so full. "We're getting another cat."

Cam chuckles into my shoulder. "We can get two more cats if you want, but not more than four."

Pointing at the attic, I whisper, "I can have that room, right? It's all I've ever wanted. An attic bedroom or office."

He kisses my neck, sending a shiver down my spine. "It's yours."

After a while of gazing and dreaming, we head back to my house.

"Just imagine the different parties we can have there. The kitchen is a dream for entertaining." I hold his hand as he drives, picturing decorating the house for Christmas. "We need to get a bigger Christmas tree."

Cam bursts out laughing. "That's like over six months away!"

"Shh," I tease. "Just picture our morning coffee on the porch as we look across the meadow. We can add a porch swing. A house like that needs a porch swing."

"We can add whatever you want." He glances over at me. "I was thinking we could build a big beautiful fire pit area, maybe sunken in with built-in seating around it."

Sighing, I smile. "I love that idea."

As we turn down my street, my house catches my eye. I frown. All the lights are on.

Cam pulls into the driveway as I ask, "Did I forget to turn the lights off?"

As we go inside, all our friends cheer, offering us glasses of champagne.

"Congrats on the house!" Elise hugs me, knowing how much I've dreamt of living there.

We're shuffled into the living room, where there's food spread out, and Mocha is perched on her cat tree supervising.

Owen comes over, nudging me. "I hope you don't mind that we invaded your space. We thought this was worth celebrating."

"The architecture on that house is stunning. I would love a tour once you're in," Young Jae adds.

"We're going to have a huge housewarming party once we've moved in, don't worry!" I'm glowing, surrounded by my friends, knowing that in no time at all Cam and I will be moving in together into the house we used to dream about together. Some of our goals together may have changed, but it makes me happy that this worked out.

I can't stop smiling as we celebrate with our friends and brainstorm details about our move, including telling Owen to keep room for us in his schedule.

After everyone leaves, I fall asleep in Cam's arms, realizing I will soon be sleeping next to him every night.

CHAPTER
Thirty-Two

RAELYNN

Taping up another box, I glance at my phone when it beeps. Rocking back on my heels, I frown. Why is my app telling me it's the last day of my period?

My stomach twists. I'm rarely late.

Bile rises in my throat, but I choke it back and send Adeline a quick text. I know she understands what I've gone through. She responds immediately with the promise of a test and chocolate.

Taking deep breaths, I work on grounding myself. The breathing helps as I work on identifying concrete things. What can I see? Hear? Smell? Touch?

Instead of feeling hopeful like every other time, I actually find myself swinging the opposite way. I've finally gotten to a good place with the direction of my relationship with Cam.

Talking myself through it, I'm muttering, "It's likely due to all the late nights I've been pulling. I've lost some weight and those things can impact my cycle. And if I am, we can handle this. I can handle this because I am capable. And we are solid. We're able to get through this."

Mocha perches on the arm of the couch, her tail twitching as I pace.

The front door opens as Adeline lets herself in, wordlessly bringing me the test.

I take the test, my jaw clenched as I head into the bathroom. The entire process takes me back to all the disappointments, and when the timer goes off, I'm vibrating. Tears are already running down my face at the mixed emotions of hope and dread building in my chest.

Flipping it over, I brace myself on the counter at the negative result. Sobs wrack my body as I crouch down to cry into my knees. The bathroom door opens, and I feel Adeline next to me.

She holds me while I cry. The only sound in the room is my gasping breaths.

"This is ridiculous. It's not like it's a surprise." Lifting my head, I meet her eyes. The sadness I feel is reflected in them. I thought I would feel relief, and it's there, but disappointment still rears its ugly head.

A tear falls down her cheek as she rests a hand over mine. "That doesn't make it any easier. Our hearts don't always match what our mind knows."

The front door opens, Cam's voice calling for me.

"We're in here." My voice is thick, and I can feel how puffy my eyes are as I look up at him.

Adeline shifts out of the way as he sees the pregnancy test and then processes my tear-streaked face.

He drops down next to me, pulling me into his arms, whispering comforting words of love into my ear.

"I'm sorry I didn't call you, I didn't want to distract you from work." My voice cracks.

Cam pulls back to press his forehead against mine. "Anytime you need me, I will be there."

Adeline excuses herself with a promise to text later. As the front door closes behind her, Cam scoops me into his arms and carries me to the couch. He settles me down, covering me with a blanket before heading to the kitchen.

Mocha jumps onto my lap, purring as she lays on my stomach.

Everything feels heavy, but I'm determined not to spiral like last time. I've come to accept that children are not part of my future, and I won't let a negative test change that. I cling to that little flicker of relief, knowing that Cam and I will have an incredible life together.

Cam comes into the room with a tray. There's a mound of chocolate and a steaming cup of tea. "I found the treats in a bag, I'm guessing Adeline brought them."

My lips quiver as I attempt to smile. "She did. I knew she had the day off, so she was the first one I thought to text. She knew exactly what I needed her to do."

He settles next to me, pulling my feet into his lap. "She's a good friend." He looks at me pensively before asking, "What do you need from me? I know we haven't been on the same page in the past."

"I just need you to be here with me. I've done a lot of work. I think I was just caught off guard. I've been so busy packing, I didn't even realize I was late until my app reminded me I hadn't input any information." Taking a deep breath, I steady myself. "I'm okay with the fact kids aren't necessarily part of our story. Taking the test threw me back, and my emotions took over."

Sipping at the tea, the warmth flows through me and I feel my heart slowly settle, my body steadying. Despite all the work I've been doing, it was so easy for me to fall back into old habits. Dr. Fletcher told me it's to be expected, but I thought I would be more prepared.

"I was using the grounding exercises I learned. What I wasn't expecting was my conflicting reaction. But even though the disappointment is there, it doesn't feel quite as heavy as it has in the past. I regressed more than I hoped I would, but it just shows that the work is ongoing." Giving him a small but genuine smile, I whisper, "I'm so glad you're here."

"I wouldn't want to be anywhere else."

We spend the rest of the day just talking and connecting. Instead of dwelling on what we can't have, I shift the focus to our new home.

"What do you think of creating a kitty wall? With ramps and little hidey holes." I pull out my phone and show him some pictures I saved.

He smirks and opens his text stream with Owen. In it are similar pictures and Owen agreeing to build something just for Mocha. "Already on it. Also, I might have gone to the shelter yesterday to drop off an abandoned bunny and went to say hi to the cats. There's an adorable gray tabby named Bruce. He's fourteen and has been there for eighteen months. I was hoping you might be on board with adopting him instead of a kitten."

Cam opens a photo, showing me Bruce, and the weight of the day falls away a little more.

"Let's go get him right now." Glancing at the time, I shove the blankets off me and stand, pulling on Cam. "They're still open for thirty more minutes."

He jumps up, pulling me into his arms and kissing me deeply. "I love you. We will create the perfect life together, I promise."

"I know. I love you too."

We make it to the shelter in record time, Brynne greets us as she comes out from the back.

"Hey guys, what can I help you with?" Brynne pushes her sleeves up, revealing her tattooed arms. Not many people know the scars those tattoos hide, but I remember seeing them once when her sleeve slipped up at school.

Looking up at her, I smile. "We're here to adopt Bruce."

Her face lights up, her eyes getting a bit glassy. "That's the most amazing news. He's our longest resident and an owner surrender. Aside from being a senior, he's in good shape now."

We follow her into the back and as soon as his yellow eyes meet mine, I'm in love. Brynne opens his cage and I scoop him into my arms, cooing at him.

"Hi, sweet baby. You're part of our family now, and you will never be alone again." He immediately starts purring and I melt.

Brynne lets me sit in the meet and greet room while Cam goes with her to fill out the paperwork.

They come back in ten minutes later and find him

curled up in my arms, eyes closed as his rattles out old man purrs.

"I'm going to waive his adoption fee. I'm just glad he has a home." She strokes under his chin, fondness clear in her expression.

Shaking my head, I refuse. "No. What you do here is important."

When Brynne opens her mouth to argue, Cam holds his hand up. "How about instead of the adoption fee, you bring anyone in that needs some dental work, and I will do it for free?"

Brynne's jaw drops, and she just nods, speechless. Cam's offer is worth more than the fee and will help so many animals. If possible, I love him even more.

We say goodbye and head home.

Less than an hour after we left, we park back in my driveway. As I adjust Bruce in my arms, I pause and worry as I see Mocha sitting in the front window. "I sure hope Mocha is as excited for him as we are."

Cam reaches over to squeeze my hand. "We will help her get there."

That evening we get Bruce set up in my office. His own space to get settled before we slowly introduce him to Mocha.

The weight of the day has eased, and while the sadness is still there, it's a manageable level mixed with acceptance.

The time spent with Cam was exactly what I needed, and as I looked at the sweet faces of the cats surrounding Bruce, who are waiting for forever homes, I realized I could give them the love I have in my heart.

After saying goodnight to Bruce, I find Mocha and give her some extra love while also letting her smell Bruce on me.

Cam cooks a late dinner, and I realize we will soon start our life together again in a new home. Our time together has been so wonderful and repaired my heart in a way I never expected. As much as our time apart hurt, I don't know if we would be where we are without it.

He turns to look at me, his hazel eyes warming me as he smiles. The promise of a life of love and happiness is unspoken between us.

Epilogue

CAMERON

Mocha bathes Bruce as they lay contentedly in the center of our bed. It's been three months since Rae and I moved into our new home and life has been everything I could have dreamed of and more.

I check to ensure I have everything before joining Raelynn in the newly built gazebo. She rocks in the swing, a book in hand, looking more content and beautiful than I've ever seen her.

My stomach is tied in knots as I watch her, a breeze blowing her curls gently. Coming home was the best decision I have ever made because it led me here. To this moment.

Taking a deep breath, I look at the woman I love more than anything in this world. The way her lips twitch as she reads, her one leg tucked up. We have laughed more, loved more, and have just been *more* since we both showed each other that we can handle the ups and downs, can handle the emotions, and be there for each other in a healthier way.

We have grown so much in these past months and I want to take it one step further.

She looks up from her book as I bound up the steps, her curls framing her face. Rae smiles at me, her expression surprised.

"I didn't hear you come home." She closes her book, shifting to make room for me.

Sitting next to her, I lean in and kiss her. "I went in to check on the cats. Mocha is giving Bruce a bath."

Showing Rae the picture I took, I can't stop looking at her as she beams.

"Those two get on better than I could've imagined possible." She gushes. She cocks her head to the side when I continue to just look at her, almost frozen because I feel so full of life.

Taking a deep breath, I slide off the bench and sink onto one knee, my heart racing as I try to put my thoughts into words. "Rae, my heart is so happy and so content. Every day I wake up and know that it doesn't matter what the day brings, we will tackle it together. Nothing in the world could make the life we're creating better, except for one thing. Raelynn, will you marry me?"

I open the ring box, revealing the blue sapphire surrounded by little diamonds. The gold band is simple, allowing the stones to be the star of the show.

Rae straightens, her feet dropping down. Her eyes glisten as she meets my gaze. "Of course I will."

Sliding the ring onto her finger, I pull her into my arms and kiss her.

She's home. She always has been and now she will forever be.

"You know how we need to celebrate, right?" she asks, her eyes lighting up as she smiles mischievously.

"Adopt a cat?"

She laughs, nodding. "You know it."

Chuckling, I take her hand. "Let's go."

Also by Ashley Erin

All Or Nothing Series
All About Us
All About Hope
All About Forever

Rule series
The No Asshole Rule
The No Bad Boy Rule
The No Jock Rule
The No Player Rule

Willowbrook Lake

By Your Side

Standalones
without walls
The Fine Line Between Love and Hate
Why Not Me?

About the Author

Ashley Erin lives in Alberta, Canada. She hates socks and wears flip flops as soon as it's above freezing. Ashley is the mother of two beautiful daughters. Her two cats and three dogs are incredibly spoiled. When she's not writing or reading; she's learning Korean, playing board games, painting, or spending time with people she cares about.

Ashley is a self-published author of contemporary and new adult romance.
For more information about Ashley Erin and her books, visit:
Facebook
Facebook Reader Group
Newsletter
Goodreads
Instagram
Website
BookBub

Manufactured by Amazon.ca
Acheson, AB

13138708R00120